I KILL THE DEAD

Life of the Dead Book 4

TONY URBAN

PACKANACK
publishing

The life of the dead is placed in the memory of the living.

— CICERO

PROLOGUE

IF YOU'RE READING THIS, I'M EITHER DEAD OR YOU'RE A NOSY bastard.

If it's the former, well, that pisses me off. I expected to be in this for the long haul. But, as I've found out often enough, death comes when we're least expecting it.

I never kept a diary before. Actually, I'm going to call this a journal. Diary sounds pretty girly.

Back to my point, if there is one. I'm not sure why I'm bothering with a journal now. I suppose I hope my story can help someone else. Maybe you can read about what I did right and what I did wrong and have a smoother ride than I've had so far. Or maybe I'm just bored. That's something I wouldn't have expected about the zombie apocalypse. Much of the time, it's really fucking boring.

I'm not the guy anyone would have expected to be in a position to give advice. A lot of people thought I was a fuck up, and shit, I am. But I'm alive, and most of them aren't, so I suppose that counts for something. Right?

For me, things started off with a scream. I was running the meat station for the afternoon buffet crowd when an old woman's husband died and came back to life. He bit some people, they started to turn, they bit some more people... You get the picture. It wasn't slow and gradual like in some of the movies. It was like someone tipping over the first in a row of a hundred dominos. One became two became three.

Click, click, click, click, click.

Before I knew it, everyone was dead but me. If I'd have made a single mistake, hesitated a second too long, or even zigged when I should have zagged, I would have become zombie chow, destined to spend eternity inside the Grand Buffet - Johnstown's #1 Budget Eatery four years running. But I made all the right moves, and I got out.

I knew the most important thing, aside from staying away from large crowds, was having the proper weapons. I didn't know much about guns and didn't trust them. Not in a pinch. So, I raided a sporting goods store and turned an unbreakable hockey stick into a dual-bladed weapon. It was long, which kept me out of arm's reach of the zombies, lightweight, and deadly as hell. It served me better than I could have ever imagined.

Initially, I had plans to head west. Out to one of those states that most people can't even point to on a map because they're so remote and sparsely populated that they're pretty much forgotten. Some place like Wyoming. That's a state, right?

Staying anywhere close to the cities was a bad move, and I knew that, but I ended up running into a big motherfucker named Bundy, and we teamed up for a while.

Eventually, we found some others. Or they found us. I guess it depends on your perspective. I thought it might be good to have a group of survivors, especially early on when we were all trying to figure shit out. More people to gather supplies, to watch your back. Strength in numbers and all that happy horse shit. Good theory, right? Well, not so much in execution.

All I wanted to do was to survive, to teach them some of the knowledge I'm going to share here. But they didn't care to listen.

They were too interested in falling in love or running around on fool's errands, trying to find missing family members who, let's face it, were almost certainly dead. Dead and walking. And eating. God, so much eating. No matter how hard I tried, they didn't listen, so one night, I hopped on my motorcycle and left their drama in the rearview mirror. I ain't got time for that.

This is the apocalypse. The end of the world, probably. But I've still got a lot of living left to do.

I'm Mead, and I kill the dead.

EARLY JULY

I's been a few weeks since I left those stupid fucking fuckers at the warehouse.

Time has not, as the saying goes, healed all wounds. I'm still pissed off at the way they acted—Ramey trading me in for Wim without a second thought, Mina going all googly eyes at fatass Bundy —and the way they treated me. Like a wad of chewing gum stuck in the tread of your shoe that you can't get rid of no matter how much you try.

Over the weeks, I've lost count of how many zombies I killed, but I know it's in the high three digits. Hell, I killed over a hundred in Cincinnati alone. I crossed Ohio, Indiana, and Illinois but turned back when I realized everything in the Midwest was flat as shit and monotonous as fuck.

I was back in my old stomping ground of Western Pennsylvania, the motorcycle careening down the highway. I won't lie, I was going way too damn fast, even if it was the end of the world and speeding tickets were a thing of the past. I'd been driving all night when I hit a rust bucket coal or steel town which was situated along a river that was grayer than a 90-year-old widow. The only reason I stopped was because more than two dozen zombies crowded my route across an ancient iron bridge.

When I'd first come across the Indian motorcycle, I'd had visions of driving into a crowd of zombies just like this one, all the while swinging my zombie-dicing hockey stick and slaughtering the monsters without so much as squeezing the brakes.

In all my travels so far, I hadn't put that plan into action, always erring on the side of safety and common sense. But that day, I was experiencing the perfect storm of boredom and rage and disappointment and general pissed off-ness that I decided to give it a go.

I was still a little unsteady on the bike, and a part of me knew the idea was mad, but I was so filled up with anger and hurt that I thought a blood vessel in my brain might explode if I didn't somehow get it all out.

I reached over my shoulder, feeling for the stick which was fastened to my back. On my first try, my fingers caught the nylon strap that held it to my body, and for a second, my hand was stuck. The bike wobbled, and I overcorrected as I tried to steady it, sending me careening to the right. Before I knew it, I was hurtling toward the barriers that marked the edge of the bridge. I jerked my hand free and got the bike back under control just in time to avoid the collision.

My heart was racing even faster than the bike. My pulse beating so hard in my ears that I could hear nothing else. I turned the motorcycle toward the zombies and picked up the pace. Fifty miles per hour. Sixty. Faster.

The wind whipped at my greasy hair, which flew out behind me like a bizarre sci-fi helmet. An actual helmet was the one thing I lacked. I'd strapped protective sports gear all over my arms, legs, and torso. I was padded up better than an NFL lineman. That was all to protect myself against the zombies—or, more specifically, their teeth.

These zombies were close enough to smell. Their sickening

sweet, putrid aroma reminded me of gone-over meat, and in this new world, that smell never failed to energize me. In a fraction of a second, the nearest zombies went from being yards away to within striking distance. I swung the bladed end of the stick as I rocketed into them.

The blade caught a zombie who wore a florescent orange highway worker's jacket in the forehead and lopped the top of its skull clean off. Chunky, black blood splashed into the air as it fell. That made me smile.

I could feel their hands grabbing at me, their fingers clawing at me as I pressed through them. I swung again and connected with the neck of a woman whose dyed red hair was piled up in a beehive above her wrinkly face. Her mouth opened in a surprised *Oh!* as her head was severed from her body. My smile turned into laughter which was impossible to hold back as her shocked, disconnected skull toppled through the air, end over end.

Next up was a short, shirtless man who was as big around as he was tall. To me, the belly button in his pendulous, gray gut made the perfect bullseye. I sliced his stomach from one side to another, and the man's intestines spilled out like dime-store candy from a burst piñata.

I slaughtered another half dozen zombies on my way through the crowd. When I emerged on the other side, I cast a glance backward, admiring the carnage left in my wake. I was pleased with myself, but there were still more of the creatures up and walking than those dead on the ground.

All my life, I had a habit of leaving things unfinished. School, jobs, being a father. If I was going to turn things around, I needed to do a complete 180, not another half-assed attempt at change. And this seemed like as good a time to start as any.

I made a slow U-turn in the road and returned to the zombies. First up was a man with a distended beer gut which was only half-covered by a Coors t-shirt. The blade caught him in the ear and arced upward, toward the split in his hair, lopping off a good twenty percent of the top of his skull.

With the boozehound disposed of, my next target was a teenage girl who I couldn't help but notice had almost perfect C-cup breasts that pushed provocatively against her Pitt t-shirt. It seemed like a real shame, but I used the stick to split her head in half horizontally.

Next, I got in a glancing blow on a young boy who looked like he was barely old enough to walk. The stick hit the toddler in the jaw and broke the hinge on the left side. It hung from his face like a macabre Halloween mask.

I was halfway through this return trip when I cut off the head of a tall, bald geezer. His oversized noggin tumbled onto the road, and I was forced to jerk the bike sideways to avoid hitting it. That proved a bad move because I steered the bike straight into the pile of intestines I'd spilled earlier. When I hit the guts, the front wheel hydroplaned, and the bike kicked to the side, propelling me straight into two zombies who were far too undead and slow to make any attempt to avoid the collision.

The bike bounced, then tipped sideways, and before I could blink, I was thrown free of it. I hit the pavement hard enough to knock the breath out of myself and skidded a full five yards. The bike went further, not stopping until it smashed into the steel fence barrier with a crunching sound that I immediately knew meant game over.

Worse still was my beloved hockey stick. I lost my grip on it when I hit the road, and all I could do was watch as the stick bounced and slid across the pavement before making a perfect hole in one as it disappeared through the fence and into the river below.

I didn't have any time to mourn my lost weapon—the perfect weapon—because even though I'd come to a stop unscathed, I did so only inches away from a lanky zombie, who looked almost like a giant from my low, on the ground perspective. The zombie snarled as it bent at the waist and reached for me.

I hopped to my feet, relieved that no parts of myself felt broken or even injured. I took a moment to congratulate myself on having the forethought to stay so well-padded and again wondered why no one else realized how helpful I could be in the humans vs. zombies war. The battle to stay alive.

I knew there was little time for ego stroking and dove into the zombie, shoulder first. I'd never played football or made a tackle, but this one was just about perfect. I connected with the creature's pelvis, driving it backward and toward the barrier at the edge of the bridge.

I felt it grabbing for me, clawing at my body, but I didn't stop until we hit the barrier. Between my low angle and the zombie's extreme height, the momentum carried it backward. Its arms flailed as it fell through the air, and I watched, grinning, as it slammed into the gray water below.

My happiness was short-lived because when I turned around, I saw the remaining zombies were within feet of me. I grabbed a buck knife from my belt, searching for an escape route, but they were all around me.

I knew I could take out a few, maybe even several, with the knife, but the blade was only good up close and personal. In a fight against more than a handful of the creatures, fighting with only a knife would be a death sentence. By the time I'd killed three or four or five, there'd be another dozen on me, and I didn't have enough padding to withstand that kind of barrage.

The closest zombie was within reach. It swatted at me, and I lashed out with the knife, severing two of its fingers. The zombie stared at its disfigured hand, curious.

The creatures were at my front, at both sides, and they were closing in. The only escape route was behind me. At my back was the edge of the bridge. And, below that, the river.

I risked a glance down at the gray water. I'd never been great at judging distance but guessed the water was a good fifteen feet below. I wasn't a very good swimmer, and the idea of jumping into that abyss terrified me.

While I looked away, a zombie moved within biting distance. It grabbed hold of my shoulder, fell into me, and chomped down. When

I turned back, I saw a zombie in a poorly-fitting polyester suit chewing on the hard, plastic shoulder pads I was wearing. Thick, opaque saliva oozed from its mouth as it gnawed away.

I was unharmed, and a little amused, but I knew time was not on my side. I rammed the knife through its eye socket, enjoying the *pop* as its eyeball burst. At first, the zombie looked up at me, its remaining eye staring in a pained "What did you do that for?" manner. Then, I gave the knife a rough twist, and the creature collapsed to its knees.

The rest of the horde was within a few feet of me. As much as I dreaded jumping, it was my only out. I climbed onto the fence, my knees shaking so hard my entire body wobbled. That was when it occurred to me that I had no clue as to the depth of the water.

What if it was only a few feet deep, and I was crushed on impact? Or what if I hit the bottom and didn't die but broke my legs? What if the current was too strong to overcome, and I drowned? Every moment that passed brought forth a new, painful worry, and I realized it wasn't getting me anywhere except closer to chickening out.

I took one more look at the zombies.

"Later, fuckers."

Then, I jumped.

It wasn't fifteen feet down. It was closer to forty, and I was wholly unprepared for the impact, landing in something between a belly flop and a face plant. I felt as if I'd taken a swan dive off a skyscraper, like all the joints in my body were dislocated at the same time. And then I was sinking.

I couldn't see anything through the polluted, gray water. The metallic taste of it filled my mouth. Flooded my nostrils. I realized fast that I needed to move. To swim. Or else I was going to die.

I kicked, but it felt pointless against the rapid rushing waters of the river and the weight of my padding dragging me further under. The irony that what was supposed to save me might now kill me wasn't lost on me. I windmilled my arms, trying to remember what I'd learned in seventh-grade gym class, but I couldn't even discern whether I was going up or down.

My lungs felt like they were full of hot coals, yet I closed my mouth like it was a vise. I didn't know how long I could hold my breath, but knew time was almost up. Maybe in more ways than one.

I tried harder to swim—or whatever frantic, desperate motions I was making with my arms and legs. I thought it was working. I was moving anyway, moving on my own now and not due to the strength of the current.

It seemed to be getting brighter around me. The water had turned from gunmetal gray to dirty dishwater. That gave me renewed hope, and I kicked harder and flapped my arms with renewed determination.

Finally, I burst through the surface, gasping for air and puking up river water at the same time. I didn't care that, along with the water, up came the remains of a few partially digested HoHos that got stuck in my scraggly excuse for a mustache. I let the river carry me along as I recovered from that near-death experience.

I was exhausted, in pain, and alone. I had no vehicle and no weapons. But I was alive. I could figure out the rest later.

I WASHED up on shore about a mile from where I made my leap of faith, and I laid there for a while, contemplating what to do next. Daylight was fading, and a night on the riverbank, which was littered with trash, including used hypodermic needles, wasn't high on my list.

After dragging myself to my feet, I grabbed a rock that had decent weight but fit comfortably in my hand and started walking. After a while, I came upon a ramshackle, ranch-style house with pea green siding and a Ford Tempo that was sixty percent metal, forty percent rust, parked in the driveway. Even though it was a bigger piece of shit than the Cavalier I'd started out this whole mess in, I thought it was the perfect solution to my current predicament.

Those hopes were dashed when I got close enough to see that the back end of the car was propped up on concrete blocks. The house wasn't much better. Three of the five front windows were boarded over, and the front door hung ajar. Nevertheless, I couldn't even see the sun above the trees, and it was better than nothing.

As I poked my head through the open door, I could barely see into the dark confines of the house, and I concentrated more on listening. It was quiet as a library, so I pushed the door open far enough to pass through.

Once my eyes adjusted, I realized the house was abandoned. There was no furniture save for a couch that looked like it had been around since World War I, complete with springs poking through the cushions. When I got close enough to smell it, I realized the aesthetics were the least of its problems. The aroma of old piss wafted from the vaguely tan fabric and punched me in the face. And as my eyes scanned the room, I discovered several plastic milk jugs filled with yellow/green liquid.

"Oh, that's fantastic."

I thought about leaving the hovel, but I supposed that, in the midst of a zombie apocalypse, I couldn't afford to be too picky.

Room by room, I checked and cleared the house. Aside from the containers of urine, the only evidence of a prior resident was a pile of dirty clothing heaped into the corner of what might have once been a bedroom, and a stained and tattered mattress sitting on the floor. I'd rather sleep in a puddle of my own vomit, thank you very much. I decided to make camp in what passed for the kitchen. Even though the old linoleum floor was filthy, it didn't smell like piss, and that was as good as it got in that place.

As exhausted as I was, sleep was slow to come, and when it did, it was restless and dream-filled. For the first time since the initial appearance of the zombies—that day that seemed so long ago at the

Buffet--I felt... not scared exactly, but at a disadvantage. I didn't like that feeling, and I vowed to fix that in the morning.

AFTER VACATING the chateau de urine, I walked another mile before coming across an old Jeep Wrangler sitting in the yard in front of a mobile home. It had no top, and the seats were torn and worn through. Four gigantic tires raised the body so far off the ground that I thought I'd have to take a running leap to get into it.

That fact made the Jeep more than a little intriguing. After all, the motorcycle had been something of an epic fail. Maybe it was time to go in the complete opposite direction. I wondered if it would even start, but the keys were missing, and further exploration was required.

I knew I was pressing my luck with a three-pound rock as my sole weapon, but I climbed the rickety wooden steps and pulled open the trailer door. The smell inside was all too familiar. It wasn't finely aged piss, though, it was death. On the floor, I spied the body of a slender woman who could have been anywhere from mid-teens to mid-sixties. It was hard to tell since her face had been eaten away to the bone.

Her body hadn't fared much better. Her breasts were mostly gone, just a few mangled lumps of blackened tissue rising from her ribcage. Her stomach was torn open, and it looked like something—or someone—had burrowed into her innards, gnawing away an irregular circle so deep I thought I could see parts of her spinal cord.

I considered clearing the trailer to see if whoever had done this to her was still around, but the last time I'd ventured into a mobile home looking for keys hadn't gone too well, and I had no desire to linger longer than necessary. I went to the kitchen and began the scavenger hunt.

As I searched through the drawers, I found a pair of scissors and decided to add them to my collection. All I needed now was paper. In the third drawer, I found a keyring with ten or more keys of various shapes and sizes. As I checked for one etched with the Jeep logo, my back was turned to the living room, where the mutilated woman had lain. And, being so caught up in examining the keys, I didn't see or hear her get up.

"Bingo!" I said as I located the Jeep key. I deposited it into my pocket, grabbed the scissors and rock, and spun around to see the dead woman rising to her feet. What remained of her insides tumbled out of the gaping hole in her belly and hit the floor with a heavy *splat* that sent coagulated, black blood splashing across the room and onto my lower legs. Undeterred by the loss, she came for me.

"You've got to be fucking kidding me."

The faceless, gutless zombie shuffled my way. Even without eyes, she somehow sensed my location. I looked at my hands, from the rock to the scissors, trying to decide which to utilize. I went with rock.

The zombie's honing beacon overcame her blindness, but it did nothing to alert her to what was coming. I strode her way, reared back with the rock, and smashed it down on her brow. Her skull crumpled inward like a dented soda can. She stumbled backward a step, then fell to her knees.

When I looked down on the wretched, dead thing, I couldn't help but feel a little sorry for it—or for its condition, anyway. But when her mouth fell open and a raspy growl tumbled out, I didn't hesitate before swinging again. This time, the rock didn't just dent her soda can skull. It smashed a hole, and the zombie crumpled to the floor, motionless once more. I stepped over her body as I fled the trailer and headed for the Wrangler.

Up close, I realized it wasn't pretty. There was no top, and the passenger door had a rust hole big enough to fit my head through. The faded, baby blue paint was pinstriped with scratches and gashes, but the big ass tires and a large, steel bumper with a forward jutting bull bar made up for the ugliness. Besides, I'm no prize winner either.

I hauled myself into the driver's seat inserted the key into the ignition.

"Start, you son of a bitch."

And it did. The Jeep fired up without any hesitation. I shifted it into gear and whomped down on the gas pedal, sending chunks of grass flying up behind me as I peeled out of the yard and onto the road.

I had a feeling I could get used to this.

JULY 6

STOPS AT FOUR DIFFERENT SPORTING GOODS STORES TURNED UP none of the amazing, unbreakable hockey sticks. I guess that was to be expected, but I was disappointed nonetheless. I was still reluctant to trust my safety, my life, to firearms, so I tossed a variety of tools into a bright, green shopping cart.

Included among them was a 36-inch axe with a lightweight composite handle. It felt good in my hands, but I missed the extra inches of length (that's what she said) afforded by the hockey stick. Nevertheless, it seemed like something that might come in handy in a pinch.

What I really needed, however, were long-handled weapons. Fighting with a single zombie up close and personal was one thing, but for even a small horde, I needed something to keep them out of arm's reach. Once they got within biting distance, the odds of survival dropped too low.

My near-death experience on the bridge made me realize once more how fast Lady Luck could change her fickle mind and say, "Fuck you, Mead. You're still a loser. Time to say sayonara." My pads were better than nothing but still exposed flesh in too many spots to be foolproof. Plus, the weight of them had almost drowned me in the river. I needed something better.

I pushed the cart full of tools and weapons through the parking lot of the plaza and spotted Tractor Supply. I thought such a blue-collar store might hold some treasures inside its walls and decided to explore.

The business was basically a farmer's version of a department store. The front half was filled with lawnmowers, tractors, weed eaters, and other lawn care machinery. As I progressed further inside, I saw pet food and supplies.

A row of plush dog toys, rubber bones, and kibble bummed me out because I'd always wanted a dog. My parents would never allow one, and once I was out on my own, none of the five or so apartments I'd rented allowed pets. Like a mutt could have really done any damage to those rat holes.

I realized I hadn't seen a single dog, or cat for that matter, since the beginning of the apocalypse, and my mood, which had been increasingly optimistic as the day wore on, took a quick detour south.

I wanted to get away from this depressing scene, but as I turned, I heard a noise I couldn't quite identify. It wasn't walking or shuffling. Scraping maybe? No, that wasn't it either. I tried to listen harder, if such an act was possible, concentrating.

Chewing? Not quite but getting warmer.

Crunching. That was it. Like someone was gnawing away at extra crispy potato chips somewhere beyond the end of the aisle.

I let the shopping cart and its contents sit and took the axe with me as I moved toward the noise. That could have been a stupid move. If the supply room happened to be teeming with zombies, a lone axe wasn't going to do me a whole lot of good. I could have been walking toward death, but the alternative was fleeing the store as a preventative measure and leaving this treasure trove of a store empty-handed. That wasn't happening.

The noise grew louder with each footstep. It was definitely crunching, and whatever was making the sound was going to town.

Another half dozen steps and I was almost there. My hands tightened on the axe handle as I steeled myself for whatever laid behind the corner. I held my breath and looked.

What I saw surprised me at least as much as anything I'd seen since the first days of the apocalypse. It was a zombie, which, of course, wasn't strange anymore, but this zombie was on its hands and knees, crouched over a ripped 50-pound bag of dog food, and had its face buried in the kibble. The chewing sound continued as it gobbled down the chow.

The scene was so bizarre, so unexpected, that I barked out a laugh and didn't even care that my cover was blown.

The zombie pulled its face free of the food, brown chunks tumbling from its jaws which still worked and chomped.

"Holy chuckle fucks. Now I've seen everything."

I must have looked tastier than generic dog food because the zombie pushed itself away from the food and turned toward me. It wore a red vest with white embroidery that read, "Gregory - Manager," and his gut was so distended from eating most of the bag of kibble that the buttons looked ready to blow.

I couldn't believe a zombie would eat dog food, but I supposed, after a few weeks trapped in the store with no human flesh to feed upon, desperation must have set in.

Greg, the manager zombie, staggered to his feet, its pendulous belly swaying back and forth like it was smuggling a five-gallon water balloon under his uniform. It took a wobbly step toward me, and I closed the gap from the other direction.

It growled at me, which seemed entirely appropriate considering its recent meal, and I thought I was probably doing it a favor when I slammed the axe into its face. The blade sunk deep into its cheek and nose with a sickening crunch, and the zombie went limp.

As I jerked the axe free from its skull, I heard an oddly musical crash nearby. I didn't hesitate, rushing toward my next target.

I found a tall, husky man in overalls and a white t-shirt tangled amongst a pile of wind chimes and weathervanes. He'd fallen to his knees, his feet ensnared in the strings and cords, and every time he moved, there came another *ding* or *dong*.

Music to die by, I thought, and I was glad I wasn't the one dying. The zombie saw me approaching and reached in my direction, but its arm was caught between decorative metal chickens, and I was in no danger.

I probably could have left him there, finished my shopping, and he'd have still been tangled up, but I wasn't in the business of taking foolish chances. I swung the axe overhead, like I was chopping a supervised piece of firewood, and slammed the axe into the top of his skull. He fell into the merchandise with another melodious clatter.

With those two finished off, I could get back to shopping. I found a rack of metal conduits in 10-foot-long sections. It was lightweight and using the blunt side of the axe, it was easy to pound the hollow ends into sharp points. To check their effectiveness, I returned to the manager and tried jamming the makeshift spear into his dead head. It plunged through his milky eye and didn't stop moving until it hit the inside of his skull. Yep, I liked this a lot. I made another half dozen of them. I'd never been a Boy Scout, but I believed in being prepared.

With weapons in hand, I knew what I needed next. Protection. In the clothing department, I found exactly that. I grabbed three pairs of jeans and they weren't the broken-in, thread-bare kind they sold in the mall for a hundred bucks a pair. These jeans were rigid and heavy and smelled of raw denim.

These were the jeans of a working man, meant to last, not look good. The denim felt almost a quarter inch thick, and I'd yet to meet a zombie that could bite through that. I added a turtleneck undershirt and a long-sleeved denim shirt, which was every bit as heavy-duty as the jeans. Putting all of this on had already made me feel more protected, but I wasn't done yet.

I found several pairs of rugged, rawhide gloves, then grabbed two pairs of steel-toed boots that fit perfectly. I took in my reflection in a body-length mirror. I thought I looked like I'd just stumbled off the family farm, and that made me think of Wim. I wondered if that oaf was still alive, and I surprised myself a little when I realized I hoped he was.

A glimpse of exposed flesh between the end of my sleeve and the beginning of the glove clued me in to the fact that I couldn't be too careful. I grabbed some duct tape and used it to connect the shirt and gloves and remove that potential weak spot, then did the same with the boots and jeans. Finally, I took the tape and ran several rows of it along the front of the shirt where the two sides were buttoned together and then made loops around my waist where the jeans and shirt met.

I felt confident that all this clothing and tape would keep me protected from the neck down, but I was already hot and working up a good case of swamp ass.

I made a mental note to grab some powder before I left the store, but first, I needed some headgear. There wasn't much to choose from, but I settled on a four-wheeler helmet with a tinted plastic face shield.

Again, I checked myself in the mirror, and that time, I couldn't find a single weak spot. I was ready to continue.

JULY 11

Even though I was armed, protected, and back on wheels, I wasn't sure what to do next. My original plan to head west still sounded reasonable, but boredom still nagged at me. Boredom and, although I'm loathe to admit it, loneliness.

I decided to head back to West Virginia to see if I could find the others. As much as their treatment of me was annoying, reteaming with them might be for the best. If nothing else, I could try to talk some sense into them. To show them what I'd learned.

Just as I started to trek south, the sky opened and dropped precipitation of the torrential variety. The topless Wrangler provided no protection, and the denim clothes soaked up the water like a sponge, so I took refuge in a pharmacy whose doors had been smashed down about the time the zombies had begun to walk.

The pill section had been the obvious target, but that didn't bother me. Sure, I'd had my share of recreational fun over the years, but there was a time and place for everything, and this was neither.

What the pharmacy did offer were shelves full of junk food, and I gorged myself until I felt like the zipper on my jeans was going to blow. That and my perennial favorite energy drinks provided all the sustenance I needed to get through several days of rain.

I also loaded up on toothpaste, toothbrushes, and dental floss. I'd been something of a fanatic about my teeth since the apocalypse started. Even something like a minor cavity could be debilitating, and the odds of finding a dentist had to be a billion to one. So, I brushed and flossed like a motherfucker.

Once the storms passed, it took me a full day to get back to that West Virginia warehouse where I'd parted ways with Wim and company. When I pulled into the parking lot and saw the vehicles gone, I knew my return voyage had been a waste of time. All that remained behind to indicate their one-time presence was a piece of yellow paper taped to the door. It read, in sloppy, oversized print:

"Mead, I'm not sure if you're coming back, but if you do, we went southwest toward Princeton. Trying to find Ramey's father. I hope you get this and catch up with us. We're better with you. Be careful and safe. Wim"

I couldn't believe the big fool, out of all of them, had thought to leave me a letter. It pissed me off and confused me at the same time. I wanted to hate Wim—I did hate him because he was the one they had all turned to for advice and comfort and protection when they should have looked to me—but unless the hayseed was putting on one hell of a show, it seemed like the farmer was the best of them. Maybe that wasn't saying much, but at least Wim cared about me. Or pretended to.

I wasn't sure if I could get past the Wim and Ramey love connection, but I was starting to realize that I wasn't as much of a lone wolf as I'd thought myself to be. I found an old roadmap in the Wrangler's glove box and unfolded it.

Princeton looked to be a few hours away. I had no way of knowing when the others had left the warehouse or if I had any legitimate chance of catching up with them, but I decided it was worth a shot. I didn't have anything better to do with my time anyway.

It was smooth sailing—or driving—until I reached a section of roadway where the asphalt disappeared, replaced with a deep chasm that looked like it had once been on fire. Charred chunks of metal and pieces of bodies littered the area surrounding it like fallen meteorites.

Bright red paint on one of the fragments caught my eye. I left the engine of the Jeep running as I jumped down to get a better look. Amidst the red paint, white backward letters read, "ulanc."

"U-lanc?" I wondered aloud, and as I said that, the sound became familiar. "Ambulance?"

Was this Mina's ride? She was a skinny, judgmental broad Bundy and I had found on the highway. She didn't like me much, and after a while, the feeling became mutual.

I knelt beside the hole in the road and could make out a broken axle and wheel. There was definitely a vehicle down there, or had been at one time anyway.

This had to be the route Wim and company would have taken. And the odds of two ambulances out and about in this remote neck of the woods were slim. But what had happened? It was like a bomb had gone off. I kicked the ulanc, and when it skittered sideways, it revealed a chunk of an arm the size of country ham.

"I'll be a son of a whore!"

In my entire life, I'd only seen one arm that possessed such impressive girth.

"Bundy."

I picked up the piece of the arm, which was slimy and dripped maggots. It must have weighed thirty pounds all by itself, and the skin felt like it was going to slough off in my hands. I was very glad to be wearing gloves. There were no identifying birthmarks or tattoos, but I knew.

"We had our differences, but I wouldn't have wished this on you, big boy." I chucked the dismembered chunk of limb into the pit.

Whatever had happened here was over and done, and I was never big into crying over spilled milk. I retreated to the Jeep, did a U-turn, and drove away.

I didn't stop driving until I came upon another roadblock. One too perfect to have been caused by a random pileup in the dawn of the apocalypse. This was manmade.

There sat Wim's Bronco, all the doors hanging ajar but with no sign of him or the others. All the many guns Wim had possessed were gone too. I thought they might have abandoned ship (or truck, as the case may be) and walked around the bizarre mashup of abandoned vehicles, but then I spotted several aerosol cans scattered across the roadway.

I lifted one and saw it was bare of writing or markings of any kind. I brought it in closer, caught a whiff, and my eyes immediately began to water. I pitched the can aside, where it bounced twice, then landed in the bushes.

I had no idea what had gone down here, but last I checked, zombies didn't use tear gas or chemical weapons or whatever shit that was. And I had no intention of finding out. I hoped the others hadn't met an end as grizzly as big, old Bundy, but this situation was well above my pay grade.

I was on my own, and it looked like it was going to stay that way.

JULY 23

I SPOTTED THE PITCHER FIRST. AT LEAST I ASSUMED THE MAN was a pitcher because he clutched a baseball in his fist like it was stuck there with superglue.

I'd been driving aimlessly since realizing my one-time companions were gone in the wind, and I thought I was somewhere in North or South Carolina, but I'd lost track. Part of me knew I should get a plan together to figure out my next move, but I was having trouble finding the motivation. Story of my life.

My main goal of late had been stockpiling as much gasoline as I could find. I was up to twelve red plastic containers in the rear of the Jeep but went through three or four of them each day. The Wrangler was a beast but a gas hog.

On the positive side, one of the good things about the current situation was that there was almost an endless supply of abandoned vehicles from which to siphon fuel. I'd even got good enough that I could spit out the tube before I got a mouthful of unleaded.

I was filling a five-gallon container when I saw the pitcher. There was a small-town baseball field ahead, and a row of four-foot-tall shrubbery lined the outfield. The pitcher bounced off the green wall and gave a frustrated growl that caused me to look up from my gas heist adventure. I watched as the pitcher made an awkward 180 and headed toward the infield.

Once the can was full, I placed it in the Jeep, then decided to check out the diamond. Before moving that way, I grabbed one of the conduit spears and the axe.

Lately, I'd mostly been ignoring zombies or running them down with the Wrangler. Its steel bumper acted like a sort of battering ram that slammed them to the pavement before the knobby 37-inch tires ran them over. Now was as good a time as any to see whether these tools could really replace my wonderful, murderous hockey stick.

Rather than climb over the hedge, I decided to stroll through the entryway to the stadium. I had to unlatch a pair of metal double doors, but after that, admittance was granted, no ticket needed.

I crossed through a small corridor which lead to the stadium. I guesstimated it could hold a few hundred fans, maybe a thousand at the most, and that would probably be standing room only. There was a scattering of trash in the bleachers, empty popcorn boxes, half-eaten hot dogs. What a bunch of pigs. And there were no undead janitors around to clean up the mess.

But my interest wasn't in the stands. It was on the field. It turned out that the Cy Young wannabe wasn't the only player to spend his afterlife on the diamond. A full roster of players, still decked out in their blue and yellow uniforms, wandered about.

To me, they looked like teenagers. Or like they'd once been teenagers. I still wasn't sure how that worked now that they'd ceased living. Were they perpetually the same age as when they died? Or do you count the time that passed? Ten years from now, would these players still be teenagers, or would they be twenty-somethings in rotting teenage bodies? I'd had too much time to think about such nonsense lately and was eager to fill my head with some good, old-fashioned killing.

I strolled around the protective netting behind home plate, then hopped over the small rail that separated the fans from the field. A pudgy boy wearing a catcher's mask was the closest to me. He didn't even see me approach from behind, and I didn't make my presence known before swinging the axe.

The blade hit the teen square in the neck, and I'd worked up enough force that the tool tore straight through. The catcher's head flew a few yards, rolling down the first base line and landing at the feet of #33, who looked down at the head, then up at me.

It was game on.

The first baseman stumbled toward me, his cleats catching in the dirt as he shuffled along. He was tall and blond, with a muscular build. I thought he looked like the type of asshole who'd made my life hell in high school, and by the time he reached home plate, I was jonesing for the kill.

The axe caught the teen in his cheek, shattering the bone as the heavy blade smashed through his face before ripping out the opposite side. It looked like a four-inch channel had been burrowed through the player's pretty face, but I had no time to admire my handiwork before the zombie hit the ground.

This felt good. I looked out to the rest of the team, which had started to amble my way. I got into a batter's stance at home plate and worked up my best announcer's voice.

"Now batting for the visiting team, Mead Myers. Mead's been on a hot streak lately and shows no signs of slowing down."

The uniform of the next player labeled him #17. He had a mop of drab, brown hair that poked out from under his cap, and he dragged along a wooden baseball bat as he walked. I thought about what a terrible weapon a bat would be when it came to fighting zombies. Too short, first of all, plus the handle was bound to break at the worst possible time. But #17 wasn't using the bat for anything more than a walking stick, so I guess it didn't matter.

I was ready to show him what a real weapon could do. I held my axe like it was my own Louisville Slugger, and when the boy was within reach, I swung for the fences.

Yep, this was exactly what I needed.

JULY 28

I WANTED TO SEE THE OCEAN. THAT WAS SOMETHING I'D NEVER done. Instead, I ended up in Baltimore, and I was none too happy about it. I'd been trying to avoid D.C., cutting through small towns and suburbs on the west side of the Chesapeake Bay, but when I hit Hawkins Point, I made a left instead of a right and, boom, next thing I knew, I was in the middle of the Charm City.

It was my biggest mistake so far, and I wanted to get out of there as quick as possible. Staying safe in a city of this size would be impossible. There were too many roadblocks. Too many places to get trapped. That was why I'd avoided the cities in the previous weeks. Safety was in the rural areas, and that was where I wanted—needed —to go.

In the parts of the city where high-rises and skyscrapers filled the landscape, the zombies were everywhere. They seemed to have been in a sort of daze until they heard the Jeep approach. That snapped them to attention, and they moved out of the stoops, off the sidewalks, and came toward me in the road.

It made me sick to see the sheer number of them, to realize the odds against me. But now wasn't the time to kill. I was one man in a city of millions of the undead. On that day, in that place, I was no longer a fighter. I was a runner.

I stopped the Jeep on a section of Martin Luther King Blvd that looked reasonably deserted and rummaged through a pile of junk food wrappers and drained energy shot bottles in the passenger footwell until I came up with my tattered roadmap. I tried to take in the street signs around me, then match them up with the corresponding place on the map but had no luck. The city was just too big, and I hadn't a clue where I was.

Then the zombie hit the door.

I don't know how I didn't see him coming, how I'd lost so much of my situational awareness as I focused on the map, but it didn't matter because he was beside me, reaching through the nonexistent window and grabbing onto my shirt.

I tried to pull free, but the zombie, a stocky, musclebound black man with a shaved head, wasn't letting go. He was tall enough that his head and shoulders extended above the door frame, even with the Jeep's massive lift. I could smell the rotten death emanating from his jaws as he snarled at me.

The axe was in the passenger footwell but leaning against the far door. No matter how hard I strained, I couldn't reach it. Nor could I reach the spears in the back seat, not with this hulk holding me. Instead, I took the atlas and used it to slap the zombie in the face. That only pissed him off even more.

Out of options, I hit the gas. The Wrangler lurched forward, and I felt the zombie lose his balance as his feet slipped out from underneath him. That transferred all his weight to my arm, and my entire body was jerked sideways where my shoulder hit the frame with a pained thud.

I could hear his feet dragging against the pavement and pressed the pedal to the floor, swerving side to side, trying to shake him free. The Jeep felt like I was riding on a wave, and I realized that any too sudden movement might not only shake off the zombie but also cause a rollover.

Ahead, I saw a postal drop box waiting at the corner. I decided it was my best hope and, with my free arm, steered the Wrangler toward it. Even through my denim shirt, I could feel the zombie's fingers digging into my skin, the weight of him straining my shoulder joint. I wondered if it was possible that he could tear my arm off. In movies, dismemberment seemed relatively easy, and I hoped that, in real life, the limbs were affixed more permanently.

As I closed in on the mailbox, I wanted to slow down, to somehow brace for the coming impact, but I wouldn't allow myself to do that. I lined up the zombie with the big blue box, and the two connected at forty miles an hour.

The zombie disappeared in an instant, like something out of a magic act. When I checked the mirror, I saw him sprawled on the sidewalk beside the crumpled and now askew mailbox. I didn't know if he was dead and didn't care. My arm and the Wrangler were free of him.

When I turned my gaze ahead, I found three zombies clustered together in the middle of the road. There was enough room that I could have avoided them, but the adrenaline was coursing through me, and I headed for the trio.

As I closed in, I realized they were grouped together so tight because they were eating someone. Their mouths tore away stringy strips of flesh. Their hands dug into the victim's skin and ripped it away greedily. The Jeep hit all of them simultaneously.

A woman wearing a black, semi-transparent skull cap careened to the right. An old codger fell in the other direction, and I felt his bones crunch under the weight of the Jeep. And straight ahead, a crouching zombie with cornrows took the blow straight on.

I expected him to fall because that's what all the other zombies I'd rammed with the Wrangler had done. But he didn't fall. His upper body burst through the push bar, and the whole Jeep shook as his torso hit the grill.

Looking out the windshield, I could see him stuck in there. His legs flailed in midair like he was trying to swim. I slammed on the brakes, expecting him to pop free, but he remained wedged amongst the bar and grill.

"You stupid fuck nugget!"

I didn't want to leave the Jeep. I felt safe inside, or as safe as it was possible to feel in that hellhole of a city. But I couldn't imagine driving around with a half-dead gut muncher protruding from the front end. I grabbed the axe, opened the door, and stepped foot in Baltimore for the first time in my life.

I heard a low gurgling behind me and looked back to see the man who was being eaten moments ago crawling on the pavement, his mouth agape in the typical zombie leer. I must have crushed his legs in the impact because he dragged himself along the roadway using only his arms. His progress was sloth-like, and I wasn't worried about that prick.

The cornrowed hanger-on was another matter. When I came around the front of the Wrangler, I saw that his upper body was twisted and contorted through the push bar. His face and shoulders were smashed against the grill. One of his hands had disappeared inside the distinctive Jeep slats, and I could smell his skin sizzling against the radiator.

He saw me coming, and his body writhed helplessly as he tried to simultaneously free himself and get me. He looked like a lost cause, but I didn't want to wait and see if he somehow managed to pull a Houdini.

I set the axe aside and grabbed his thrashing legs, pinning them under my armpits. It reminded me a bit of a childhood game we played once at church camp, something about a wheelbarrow. I didn't remember many of the details because I rarely partook in the festivities since I never had luck finding a partner.

I pulled on his legs, trying to squeeze him free. He didn't budge. I took a deep breath and jerked harder, throwing myself backward. Still, there was no progress.

"Motherfucker, get out of my Jeep!" A third attempt ended in equal failure.

Fed up, I grabbed the axe handle. If this bastard wasn't coming out whole, he was coming out in pieces. My only worry was missing and chopping the Jeep, but I aimed carefully.

The first blow struck the zombie in the side, cutting open his love handle. Another chop went an eighth of the way through his midsection. I could tell this wasn't going to be an easy job.

It must have taken ten solid minutes of hacking away, and I was sucking wind so hard I thought my lungs might collapse. Chunks of flesh, bits of chopped-up organs, and pints of blood covered the Jeep, the road, and me.

Finally, I was all the way through the zombie's torso. His intestines had fallen free, slithering and looping themselves around the push bar and bumper like gory streamers.

Now, when I grabbed his legs and pulled, they extracted themselves easily. I dropped them to the pavement, where they looked like a dirty, discarded pair of pants.

During the ordeal, the zombie never stopped growling and groaning. If anything, his desperate cries seemed to escalate. I saw him watching me as I got closer with the axe. His upper body was still entwined in the front end, and his face twisted up in a snarl as I approached.

"Fuck you too!" I smashed the top of the axe into its face and heard teeth break. When he opened his mouth, he looked like he had a maw full of partially eaten chiclets, and that made me laugh a little.

I hooked the axe head around his neck and pulled. He moved, slowly at first, but then the lubrication from the blood aided in the dislodgment, and the top half of the zombie flopped onto the road face first. I didn't bother with the axe. Instead, I slammed my foot against the back of his skull and drove it into the macadam.

Exhausted, I leaned against the hood of the Jeep to catch my breath. And that's when a new zombie grabbed me.

Fingers caught the back of my shirt, jerking both it and me upward. The fabric dug into my neck, hitting my windpipe and making me cough. I was already having trouble breathing, and this wasn't helping matters at all.

I was dragged backward a foot, then two, and I could smell the rancid cologne of death as the creature pulled me toward him. I'd had the good sense to wear my helmet, and I threw my head backward. I felt a jarring impact as the helmet collided with bone, and the hand that had been holding me let go of my shirt.

When I spun around, I found a hulking zombie with long dreadlocks that hung past his shoulders. His dark skin had taken on an ashen pallor, and his eyes were a matching shade of gray. He was an easy foot taller than me and probably fifty pounds heavier. And he wasn't just huge and angry. He was coming for me again.

"Goddamn, I hate this city."

As soon as he was in striking distance, I pounded the axe into his face. The blade destroyed his jaw, but I'd swung a fraction of a second too soon, and all the damage was superficial. Shards of teeth and gums tumbled from his mouth and onto the pavement. He groaned but was ready for round three.

I wasn't. I didn't even have enough time to raise the axe again before he was on top of me. All I could do was spin out of the way and let him stumble into the Jeep.

I swung the axe, aiming for the base of his skull but couldn't get enough height and buried the blade in his upper back instead. His arms flailed, clumsily trying to reach for the weapon but having no luck. I yanked on the axe, trying to free it from its newfound sheath, but I wasn't having much luck either, and the handle slipped free from my grip.

The zombie managed to turn around, the axe handle banging off the body of the Jeep, and he was on the move yet again. The only asset I had on my side was that I was nimbler, or at least not a clumsy, undead bastard. I darted away from him, toward the back of the Jeep, and grabbed one of the conduit spears.

He was a yard away and closing in fast. I scrambled into the back of the Wrangler, ready to leap into the driver's seat and speed away.

Ready to abandon the axe and the zombie, but I was annoyed, and I wanted to finish this fucker off for good.

Inside the vehicle, I had the height advantage, so when the zombie hit the tailgate, I had the perfect angle to drive the spear into him. I reared back, then thrust it forward, connecting it with the center of his forehead.

And the spear bounced off.

That's the thing with zombies. It's not like the movies where their heads are made of paper mache. Their bodies aren't any different from yours or mine. Their skulls are still really fucking hard. Sure, the spear opened a nice gash that would have taken an assload of stitches to close, but I'd be surprised if it made so much as a scratch in his bones. And it really pissed him off.

"Fuck this."

I didn't need this shit. I bounced into the driver's seat, threw the Jeep in reverse, and knocked the zombie to the ground. I rolled all the way over him and didn't stop until I could see him through the windshield.

He was sprawled on the road, face up. I couldn't tell if he was dead for sure, but he wasn't moving. And the axe—my axe—had been knocked loose. It laid on the road between me and the zombie.

I should have driven away. I knew that, but I'm not perfect, and it was a matter of principle. I again left the Wrangler.

It was only five feet to the axe but felt like fifty. I didn't take my eyes off the man as I crouched down and retrieved the weapon. As I stood back up, the zombie groaned.

This bastard had already caused me a week's worth of grief, and I was more than happy to put an end to the day's drama. I aimed more carefully this time and struck with the spear.

It hit just below his eyeball, sinking deep into the socket. In the process, his eye was pushed free, popping out like a champagne cork. It rolled down his cheek, dangling off the side of his face.

"Take that, shit face."

The spear was in so deep I had to put my foot on his chest for leverage to free it. But it was over. Or so I thought. I grabbed the axe and moved toward the Wrangler.

"Drop that axe, cracker."

The voice was behind me. It was tight and either excited or angry, or both.

"Stay calm," I said and turned slowly toward the sound of this new arrival, not knowing who awaited me. Again, I cursed myself for ending up in Baltimore.

When I made it 180 degrees, the first thing I saw was a gun barrel aimed at my face.

"I told you to drop that axe, yo," the man with the pistol repeated. "And whatever that thing is you just used to kill O'Dell."

The man was in his mid-twenties with thick gold chains dangling from his neck. So many that he conjured up an image of a skinny version of Mr. T. He was so lean that I suspected I might be able to take him in a hand-to-hand fight, but even armed with an axe and spear, I wasn't about to tangle with a man with a gun, so I dropped both to the roadway and took a step away from my weapons.

"There you go. I've got no beef with you, so don't shoot me."

"Take off that helmet."

I did as ordered, and the man with the pistol lowered it a few inches. Now, it wasn't aimed at my face but more in the general direction of my gut. Better, but not much.

The man looked at the carnage around me, eyes twitching. "Why'd you go and kill O'Dell?"

I tried to follow his gaze. In the sea of corpses, it was hard to discern which of the zombies the man was talking about. He tucked the gun into the waistband of his jeans as he strode toward me and the bodies.

"He was my homeboy." He knelt beside the huge, deadlock-sporting zombie that had caused me so many headaches and rested his palm on top of the dead man's bloody forehead, careful to avoid the expelled eyeball.

I watched in uncomfortable silence. I wanted to extricate myself from this situation as quickly and safely as possible.

When the gunman removed his attention from the zombie, he turned it my way. "Why the fuck you gotta come to the city and kill my zombies? Don't you got enough zombies in whatever cracker-ass Podunk hick town you rolled in from? Where the fuck you from anyway? Cumberland?"

"Western P.A. actually."

"Shit, yo, that's even worse. So, what's your deal? You some kinda KKK motherfucker who think it'll be fun to go the hood and kill some niggas? Kill O'Dell?"

That was the last thing I wanted. "I got lost. I didn't even mean to drive in to the city. I was trying to avoid it. Really."

"Well, you did a sorry ass job of that."

"No shit." I gave a nervous, twitchy smile and hoped the man would reciprocate it. He did not.

"Fucking crazy white people." The man stood, shaking his head. "Who the fuck are you anyway? Denim Dan?"

"My name's Mead."

"Now that's a cracker name if I ever heard one."

"What's yours?"

"LaRon."

His anger seemed to have faded. I took a chance and pushed my hand LaRon's way. I was more than a little surprised when he accepted. "I'm still pissed at you for killing O'Dell."

"He was going to eat me."

LaRon took a sad look at his fallen friend. "Yeah, he do that now." He turned back to me. "What's with the Canadian tuxedo?"

Again, I was confused, and he must have seen it on my face.

"Your clothes, fool. You look like you just robbed the Levi's factory or some shit."

"Oh." I smiled, relieved to understand the question and a little excited to be able to share my ideology. "It's for protection. They can't bite through the denim. And the tape, that's to keep everything tight together so they can't pull up my sleeve or pant leg and get me."

LaRon stared for a moment, then nodded. "You a clever motherfucker, ain't you?"

I nodded. I was indeed a clever motherfucker.

"Where you headed?"

I thought about lying since the truth was so lame, but I couldn't think up an alternative quick enough. "I guess it'll sound kind of stupid, but I wanted to see the ocean. I've never been there, so I was heading to Jersey."

LaRon grinned and revealed gold-capped teeth. "Shit, yo. You want to get the ocean experience, you gotta go to Ocean City."

"Oh. All right." I would have agreed with almost anything to keep the man with the gun in a good mood.

"You drive, I'll lead the way."

I was shocked and a little alarmed over the idea of taking this stranger, this gangster, along for the ride. "You want to go with me?"

"Why not? I got nothing to do here. And besides, you're the first living motherfucker I've seen since shit got real."

That last part surprised me. I would have expected more survivors in a city the size of Baltimore. Adding that to my own anecdotal experiences of seeing no one alive since I left Wim's group, and I had to wonder how lethal the plague had been. Before I could make a comment along those lines, LaRon hopped into the Jeep, and any ideas I had of leaving him behind were put to an end.

"Drive me back to my crib first. Let's load this bitch up if we're gonna take a road trip."

"Where do you live?"

"Over on Lexington by the po house."

I decided there was no sense protesting and resumed my spot behind the wheel. "You tell me where to turn."

"You got it."

THE SIGN on the red brick building read, "Home of Edgar Allen Poe," and then it made sense. I almost laughed. "Oh, you really meant the Poe House."

"What the fuck you think I meant?"

I chewed on my lip, not wanting to say what I'd thought.

"You think I meant poor? Shit yo, if that the case, everywhere around here be the po house."

That was exactly what I'd thought he meant. The buildings all appeared decrepit and unkempt. The sidewalks were broken and crumbling. The area looked like it had been uninhabited, not for weeks but years. Like the apocalypse had come to this part of Baltimore a decade earlier than the rest of the country.

LaRon unlocked the front door to one of the crumbling rowhouses and pushed it open. He took a step inside, then looked back to me. "What you waiting for? I ain't a zombie. I don't bite."

He disappeared inside, and I followed. If he was going to murder me, I assumed he'd have done it on the street, not in his home. After all, there was no one around to arrest him if he'd have shot me in broad daylight.

The apartment smelled like someone had unloaded an entire canister of marijuana-scented air freshener, and I thought I might get a contact high just from breathing. After weeks of energy drinks and junk food roller coasters, that might not be a bad thing.

When I looked around the apartment, I saw stacks of cash and a smorgasbord of drugs. Most of it looked untouched, still wrapped tight in plastic, but a three-foot by three-foot cube of marijuana had been cut open, and a sizable chunk was missing. That made sense, considering the aroma. And it also made sense that the armed man with the gold grills was a drug dealer.

LaRon tossed his pistol onto a leather couch, and I instinctively flinched.

"You sure are a jumpy motherfucker."

"I've never been around guns. Guess they make me a little nervous."

"Shit, man, you said you're from Pennsylvania. I thought they gave you a gun as soon as you came outta yo momma's womb. Besides, I ain't had ammo for that since the day after all this zombie shit went down. Only way it's gonna hurt you is if I pistol whip your ass."

The realization that I'd been cowed by a man with an empty gun annoyed me, but I supposed it was only fair. After all, I did have an axe, and I had killed O'Dell.

"Chill out, yo. Sit down and stop acting all twitchy. You're making me nervous."

I might have been twitchy, but I was also exhausted from that earlier battle. I took his advice and flopped down in a recliner as LaRon disappeared into a bedroom. I spied an unsmoked joint on the table and wondered if the man would mind if I borrowed it. He had told me to chill out after all. I leaned toward it, reaching, when LaRon reentered the room.

"You stealing my shit now? That how this is gonna work? I invite you into my home, and you steal my weed?"

"I—" Fuck! Why did I even come here?

LaRon grinned. "Shit yo, it's aight. I'm just bustin your balls. If anyone ever needed some weed, it was you." He fished through the pockets of his baggy jeans, pulled out a lighter, and tossed it my way.

I needed a joint now more than ever, so I grabbed it and fired up. LaRon nodded approvingly. "My man."

I couldn't remember the last time I'd smoked pot, but it was a year or more. My meager wages at the Buffet had barely been enough to pay my rent and bills. Every dime I made went toward necessities. There wasn't any left over for such recreational activities.

It amused me to realize that money was now useless. Hundred-dollar bills? May as well use them to wipe your ass.

LaRon reached over, and I passed him the joint. He took a hit and blew smoke rings into the air. "Good shit, huh?"

I nodded. It was indeed good shit. Much stronger than anything I'd previously tried, and it loosened my lips. "So, you were what, a drug dealer? What was that like? Fun?"

LaRon glanced at the drugs that filled the corner of the apartment and shrugged his shoulders. He returned to the bedroom, where I could see him filling a duffle bag with clothing. "Always thought of myself more as an entrepreneur. Business is all about supply and demand. Ain't no different on the streets. My merchandise just happened to be drugs. And I kept my customers happy."

He glanced at me through the open doorway. "What about you? What'd you do before all this shit?"

"I was a line cook. For a couple months anyway. Before that, I worked on an assembly line in a warehouse. And before that, I mowed lawns part-time."

"You a regular jack of all trades."

"I wasn't career-oriented, I guess you'd say."

LaRon returned to the room, took another puff on the joint, and handed it back to me. "I got you. I got you. All them stupid fuckers wasting their life away on nine to fives, where'd it get em? Out there, wandering around, dead as shit. Trying to find someone to eat, but there ain't hardly no one left. Joke's on them."

I hadn't thought of it that way. The dead outnumbered the living ten thousand to one, if not more. That didn't leave much food to go around. It was a wonder anyone had survived those odds. "How'd you stay alive?"

"Stayed in here for the most part. Night it started, some little nerdy fucker came running at me, said his kid needed to get to the hospital. So, I rounded up O'Dell, and we motored that way. Next thing you know, the kid's biting on O'Dell like he got rabies. After that, it all went to hell, you know?"

I knew all too well.

"The first night was the worst cause I didn't know what the fuck was going on. Had soldier types setting buildings on fire and shit. Riots where the popo were shooting people for no reason, even shooting the white folk. Then dead people coming back to life. I figured it out fast enough then. Came back here, bolted the door, and decided to put some of my inventory to use. If I was gonna die, I may as well be high, right yo?

"Only morning came, and I was still alive. I went out a couple times to load up on food. And try not to be food. But I've been in here 99 percent of the time."

LaRon grabbed a few framed photographs off a coffee table. Most depicted him as a younger man, photographed standing beside or embracing a woman I assumed to be his mother. One was of him and the man I now knew to be O'Dell. LaRon added them to the duffle bag and zipped it closed. "Got all I need. Ready to bounce?"

I was.

JULY 29

The boardwalk at Ocean City was almost empty, and that surprised me. It was the middle of summer, and in my mind, it seemed like there should be tourists everywhere. It took me a few moments to remember the plague had hit in early May, before the summer travel season. Before school was out and families ventured to places like this for their once-a-year reprieve from their boring, work-filled lives.

As I drove the Jeep onto the wooden planks that separated the roads and parking lots from the beach, I ran down a middle-aged woman in a sundress. Ahead of us, five zombies shuffled and stumbled through the dense sand.

"Think you can handle them?" LaRon asked as he opened his door and hopped down from the Jeep. He grabbed an aluminum baseball bat he'd brought along.

I nodded. I'd certainly taken out groups much larger than this. "Sure thing."

"Good. I'm going shopping." With that, LaRon was gone, bounding onto the boardwalk, where he disappeared among the bodegas and kiosks.

The closest zombie was only a few yards away. I floored the gas, and the Wrangler bounced down from the boardwalk and onto the beach. The tires sprayed sand from behind in a way that made me think of snow from a snow blower.

The Jeep smashed into the zombie, an older woman with dyed black hair, and sent her careening into the sand. The tires rolled into her, and the *pop* as her body exploded underneath drowned out all other sounds. If you've ever seen roadkill where they're all burst apart and there's blood everywhere and their guts have burst out their asshole and wondered if that happened with people too, it does. And it did.

A burst of wet, black blood splattered the driver's side door and window, and some even rained down on me through the open roof. I was glad I had the whole ocean to wash off in.

I continued along the beach, running down the other zombies as I came to them. By the time it was finished, the Jeep was dripping gore. That was fine. It was never going to win any beauty contests anyway.

I returned to the approximate area where I'd dropped LaRon, but the man was nowhere to be seen. I wasn't too worried, though. If LaRon had survived weeks in Baltimore, he should be able to handle a few minutes in nearly deserted Ocean City.

I took my axe as I exited the Wrangler—I couldn't be too careful. As soon as my feet hit the beach, my shoes filled with sand. I could feel it working its way underfoot, the hard grains between my toes. It was uncomfortable, but at the same time, I enjoyed it because it was so unique and different from anything I'd experienced before.

That made me realize just how little I'd lived in my almost thirty years. Shit, most of my life, I was barely five hours away from the ocean, and I'd never so much as felt sand on my feet until that day. How many other things had I been missing out on?

By the time I got to the water, even its gray coloring appearance couldn't have dampened my excitement. In the movies and on the travel TV shows, the water was clear and blue and sparkling. This looked like a never-ending seascape of dirty dishwater.

Nonetheless, it was amazing. I loved all of it. The damp breeze blowing against my cheeks. The soft but steady splashing of the incoming waves. And especially the smell, which was free of death.

"What's wrong, yo?"

I turned and saw LaRon just a few feet away. The man had two large plastic bags filled with unseen merchandise, and he stared at me with curiosity.

I hadn't realized I was crying until that very moment and wiped my eyes with the back of my hand. "Nothing."

LaRon grinned. "It's alright, man. For all we know, we're the last two people in all of Maryland left alive. It's ninety degrees. The sun's shining. Life's pretty fucking grand, ain't it?"

"Yeah, it is."

LaRon set the bags on the sand and crouched down beside them as he sifted through the contents. Soon enough, he came away with a small, silver camera. He raised it to his face.

"Say cheese, motherfucker."

I barely had time to react before the man snapped my photo. LaRon looked at the display screen and cackled.

"Let me see." I reached for it, but LaRon held it over his head, easily keeping it away from me.

"Not yet. One more where you don't look so damn goofy."

"Alright." I crossed his arms and gave an awkward smile that came off more as a sneer.

LaRon laughed again. "Guess that's as good as it gets."

He handed over the camera, and I checked the images. Jesus, did I really look like that? I'd gotten so fat over the last few weeks. Better cut down on the Twinkies and Ding Dongs. Despite that, seeing my image and the never-ending ocean in the background made me grin.

"Your turn." I pointed the camera at LaRon, who held his hand up.

"Gimme a sec." LaRon stripped off his shoes, socks, shirt, and jeans, leaving behind just his striped boxers and gold chains. His lean body was covered in black tattoos. He flexed his right arm and aimed his left toward the sky like some sort of Greek God. I took his picture, then handed the camera to him.

LaRon gave a wide smile, pleased. "Damn, that's a good-looking brotha."

"Indeed," I agreed. "Now, how are we going to get them printed?"

LaRon shrugged his shoulders. "Hell if I know. But I got us a shitload of batteries and memory cards out the ass, so we should be good for a long while."

He tossed the camera back to me, then bounded through the sand and into the frothy surf. I took a few more photos of him in the process.

"Shit yo, the water's perfect! Get your pasty ass in here!"

Even though I'd been planning this for days, I hadn't had the forethought to secure swim trunks. Under the circumstances, I doubted it mattered. I stripped down to my briefs and followed my new friend into the ocean.

THE SUN HAD DIPPED below the horizon, and the cool breeze coming off the ocean made goosebumps rise on my skin. I didn't do much actual swimming. My near-death experience in the river still had me wary. But even doing nothing more than bobbing around in the water all day had sucked the energy from my body, and I felt as if I could fall asleep at any moment.

I didn't want to sleep, though. I was so high on life (not the marijuana that LaRon eagerly smoked) that I didn't want to let that happen and bring the day to an end. I'd never felt so alive and free. I wanted to feel that way every day, and my mind raced with ideas for new experiences.

"Did you ever make a bucket list?" I asked.

LaRon laid on his back in the sand, staring up at the sky as it made its slow transition from purple to black. He raised an eyebrow, skeptical or curious or both. "The fuck's a bucket list?"

"A list you make of things you want to do before you die. Like climb Mount Everest or take a hot air balloon ride."

"Sounds like a white folk kinda thing. We don't got time for that. My bucket list was not getting shot every day."

"Yeah, but what I mean is, we have no responsibilities. No one to answer to. We can do anything we want, man. Anything. Isn't there something you've always wanted to do but never had the chance?"

As I looked to LaRon for a response, I saw a zombie approaching from behind. It was about twenty feet away and making slow progress through the sand. I wasn't in a hurry either.

LaRon rolled onto his side, white sand clinging to his ebony skin. His brow furrowed as he considered it. Then he smiled. "I always wanted to fuck Kylie Jenner. Does that count?"

I barked out a laugh. "Yeah, I guess. But it's a little late for that."

"Maybe not. She could still be alive. And even if she ain't, I never been too picky."

That made me laugh even harder. LaRon joined in. Our combined noise drifted across the beach and caused the zombie to pick up its pace.

"I was thinking, though, if what we've seen so far holds true, there are maybe a few thousand people left alive in the whole country. Probably a lot less, really."

"You're killing my buzz, Mead."

"I don't mean it like it's a bad thing. I mean, I guess maybe it is. But it doesn't have to be. There's enough food and drinks around to last the rest of our lives. Probably tenfold. We don't have to work. Don't have to answer to anyone. In the history of mankind, I bet people have never been this free."

The zombie had halved the distance. I didn't want to interrupt this mostly one-sided conversation, but I reached beside myself and took hold of the axe, still not standing up.

"So, what do you wanna do?" LaRon asked. "See the Grand Canyon or something?"

"Maybe, but not yet. First, I want to see Stephen King's house."

LaRon cocked his head. "The writer guy?"

I nodded, stood, and pointed behind LaRon. "Hold that thought."

LaRon turned and watched as I circled around him, moving toward the zombie. It was a young woman in denim shorts and a "Virginia is for Lovers" retro t-shirt. Her brown hair was clumped together and swayed from the back of her head like a heavy rope. When I closed in on her, she gasped, and a trickle of brown drool seeped from her open mouth.

I didn't hesitate. I swung the axe, and the blade struck her in the temple. The force snapped her neck, and her head flopped to the side. She fell fast, pulling the axe handle from my hands when she hit the beach. I yanked it free and let the lapping waves gradually pull her body away.

Finished, I turned back to LaRon. "Yeah, the writer."

"That dude's creepy as shit."

I smirked. "I've read all his books. Seen all the movies. And I always wanted to see his house. I saw pics online. He's got a gate with spiders and gargoyles. It's incredible."

"Where's it at?"

"Maine. I even know the street name."

"Are you a stalker or something?"

"You ever see *Misery*? I'm his biggest fan."

LaRon chuckled. "You're such a damn nerd. Ain't Maine practically in Canada?"

"Damn close."

LaRon flashed his gold-capped teeth in a Cheshire cat grin. "Then I guess we're going to Maine."

I was surprised but thrilled that he'd acquiesced so easily. He extended his fist, and I gave it a corresponding bump.

I did the numbers in my head. I knew where Maine was on the map and tried to guess how far we'd need to travel. I thought it must be well over a thousand miles. "It's a long drive. We'd be smart to stock up on weapons."

"We should steal a motherfuckin tank. Talk about ridin dirty."

He laughed when he said that, but I didn't. A tank definitely sounded interesting. And it occurred to me that I might know where to find one. Besides, as I'd asserted earlier, there was no one to stop us from doing whatever the hell we wanted to do.

"We should take a little detour first," I said.

"Whatever you say, Mead. But let's wait until the morning."

LaRon laid in the sand. I knew sleeping out in the open wasn't the smartest idea, but I had a feeling that, for once in my life, luck was on my side.

JULY 30

A BRICK-ENCASED SIGN DECLARED THE BUILDING "Pennsylvania National Guard Armory," and a neighboring plaque warned "U.S. Property - No Trespassing." I ignored both as I steered the Jeep into the empty parking lot.

The plain, concrete block building that stood behind the lot was nondescript, with a few industrial windows and only two glass double doors on the front side to permit entrance. To the right, under a steel canopy, stood a row of five tan tanks that would have looked more appropriate in the Middle East than in Western Pennsylvania. All that was separating us from the parking lot was an eight feet tall chain link fence.

"Holy shit, man. You wasn't joking," LaRon said as he bounced in the passenger seat with excitement.

I smirked, quite pleased with both myself and the reaction from my new friend. "I drove by this place every day for three years when I lived in Friedens. Never gave it a thought, really."

I parked the Wrangler about ten yards from the fence, then moved to the front end and pulled the steel cable of the winch loose. Some bits of dried gore from my zombie encounters clung to the wire, but I ignored that as I looped the line around one of the metal fence poles and a chunk of fencing, then turned to LaRon.

"There's a toggle switch by the lights. Flip it." I watched as LaRon found it and hit it.

The slack was pulled from the cable as it tightened. When it was taut, the metal of the fence gave a low creak. It yawned outward, toward the Jeep, the pole bending, screeching. Then, it gave a metallic *twang* as the pole snapped off. After that, it was easy peasy as the fencing came apart and a hole more than large enough to walk through opened.

LaRon shut off the winch and jumped down from the Jeep. "You rednecks have the best toys."

"I'll take that as a compliment." I held down the fencing with my foot so that LaRon could pass through, then followed.

The hatch to the tank was easy enough to open, and I felt truly accomplished and successful for one of the first times in my life. That feeling faded somewhat when I was unable to squeeze my newly chunky frame into the opening. That was okay, though, because LaRon had no problem fitting inside.

Once there, he looked up, confused. "Yo, how do we start this bitch?"

"Isn't there a key or something?"

"Nope. No keys. I don't even see a hole for one. I thought you knew what you were doing with this shit?"

My smile faded along with my confidence and all my feelings of accomplishment. I turned away from LaRon, my eyes cast at the ground, and wondered how I could have been so damn stupid.

So, maybe a tank wasn't the best idea, but that didn't mean the whole detour had to be a bust. This was a freaking armory, after all. There had to be something useful inside.

After using the winch to tear open the double doors, our search of the building proved a goldmine. There were dozens of rifles and pistols with matching ammunition, knives, grenades, and more than a few weapons I couldn't identify by sight. Truth be told, I didn't know how to use most of them, but that was okay because LaRon clapped me on the back.

"You done good, Mead. You done real good."

His knowledge of firearms far exceeded my own, and he rattled off brand names and model numbers like he'd been cramming for a test. We loaded up whatever we could carry and fit into the rear of the Jeep.

Along the way, I discovered two swords mounted on a wall. They hung beside a black and white framed photo of some soldiers that looked straight out of a Civil War reenactment. I thought they might be decorative, but when I pulled one out of the scabbard and swung the blade at a flag pole, the sword easily halved the inch-thick wood. I liked this better than the axe. It was longer and lighter. It still wasn't my hockey stick, but things were looking up.

We were almost finished when LaRon pointed to a nondescript, gray door. "What you think they're hiding in there?"

To me, it looked like it might lead to a janitorial supply closet. "Mops and brooms would be my guess."

LaRon tried the knob. It was locked, and he raised an eyebrow. "They lock up mops and brooms but leave enough guns to arm Al-Qaeda free for the taking?"

That was a good point. "I'll look around for keys."

I turned down a small hallway but only made it a few feet before I heard three rapid gunshots. I turned back to see LaRon holding a pistol with smoke wafting from the barrel and the doorknob blown to pieces.

"Don't need no keys, man."

He was right, of course. I was still in the process of adjusting to this new, lawless society where you could have anything you wanted if you had a sack big enough to take it.

I returned to LaRon, who pulled open the door, careful to avoid the razor-sharp shards of metal the bullets had created. I was at his side as the door came open. When the contents were revealed, I was confused, but LaRon grinned so big that it looked like his face might split.

"What is it?" It was a gun. I knew that much. But it looked like an antique, or better yet, a movie prop. It had multiple copper barrels that were shined to such a high gloss finish that I could see my own distorted and even fatter-than-usual reflection. At the other end was a hand crank of some sort.

LaRon clapped me on the shoulder. "It's a Gatling Gun. Old school shit, Mead, but I think it's the answer to all our prayers."

I thought that term, Gatling Gun, sounded familiar. Like something from a Wild West movie, but that was the problem. My knowledge of firearms didn't extend much beyond popular culture. I bet Bundy would have known all about this relic. And if LaRon was this excited, Bundy probably would have been shitting a brick. Hell, he might have even owned one. The giant—R.I.P.—had been a cranky bastard, but he sure knew his guns.

"You know any auto body shops around here?" LaRon asked.

I thought I remembered there being one a few miles up the road and nodded.

"Then help me load this bitch up and take me there. I got an idea."

WE ROLLED into Don's Collision Center, where the parking lot was vacant aside from a few crashed cars and trucks that sat waiting for repairs that would never come. LaRon shot open the locked door, then poked his head inside.

"Empty."

He disappeared into the building, and a moment later, one of the garage bay doors opened. LaRon waved me forward. "Pull the Jeep inside."

"Why?"

"Don't ask. Just do it. I ain't let you down so far, have I?"

He had not, and I obeyed, but not before noticing that the sounds of the gunfire, coupled with the Wrangler's engine, or both, had drawn the attention of some zombies that mulled around a gas station and mini-mart across the street.

Once inside the open bay, I shut off the engine. "Now what?"

"I'm gonna need an hour or two," LaRon said as his eyes scanned the variety of tools, auto parts, and sheets of metal.

I could tell the man had a plan and had no interest in distracting him. Besides, the mini-mart zombies were in the process of crossing the street and heading our way. I grabbed one of the swords and headed back into the parking lot.

The nearest zombie was a teenager, probably just old enough to drive. He wore a camo sweatshirt, a camo baseball cap, and blue jeans that were as much mud brown as indigo. I strolled toward him, and the two of us met at the edge of the lot. The camo-clad zombie swatted at me, then growled when I dodged his clumsy attempt.

"Like your outfit," I said as I raised the sword. "Almost didn't even see you there."

The zombie lunged toward me, jaws chomping, and I responded by driving the tip of the sword into its open, almost expectant, mouth. It reacted with a choking, gurgling gasp, and black blood oozed from his lips.

I whipped the sword sideways and opened its cheek. Through the gaping wound, I could see a few stained, half-rotten teeth, but I didn't take time to study them, instead swinging the sword in a back-handed motion, catching the teen in the ear. The blade sliced off the top third of it, then sunk deeper into its skull. With that, whatever had been keeping the zombie mobile was gone, and it collapsed to the ground.

There were three more zombies coming toward me. A tall, burly creature with a beard that would have been scary when he was alive and was even more so now since he was not led the way. Its wiry, brown hair was clumped with dried blood, and I could see bits of decayed flesh residing in it, giving it the appearance of some type of wild animal's nest.

When it got close enough, I saw something else in that beard. Something alive and writhing. Maggots had been birthed in that fury abode, and they feasted on the chunks of partially eaten flesh that clung to the beard.

The sight of the tiny, white worms slithering through that hair, eating that dead tissue, made my stomach flip, and I clamped my mouth shut to prevent myself from barfing. That was it. I'd had enough of this freak show, so I drove the sword into the bearded zombie's eye socket.

Next up was a young girl, maybe ten or so, and I thought she had the same pale green eyes as maggot beard. I wondered if she had been his daughter but didn't pause long to consider it. One strong swing with the sword cut straight through her head, cleaving it just below the bridge of her nose.

The top third of her skull flipped through the air and came to a rest at the feet of the last remaining zombie, a skinny, old woman wearing a teal sweatshirt that read, "World's Greatest Gramma." I watched as Gramma's foot came down on the dead girl's head. Like something out of the *Three Stooges* movie, she lost her balance, arms flailing, and careened sideways before hitting the pavement with an audible thud.

I moved to her side as she attempted to get up, and when I peered into her small, lifeless eyes, she hissed at me.

"Yeah, I don't like you much either." I stabbed her in the ear and was surprised when the blade continued the whole way through and poked out from the other side. I really liked this sword.

I LEFT LaRon to whatever he was doing in the garage and crossed the street to the mini-mart. The top hinge on the door was broken, and it hung open crookedly, granting me easy access.

At first, I thought the store was empty, but when I ventured deeper inside, I heard a low grumble. I clenched the sword tight as I moved toward the noise, which seemed to be coming from the checkout area.

As I got closer, I heard scratching and clawing, and then a rack of cigarettes tumbled over. That elicited another growl. It sounded annoyed. Almost human. But not.

I had to remind myself of that from time to time. No matter what the zombies looked like. No matter how they reacted or what noises they made, the stuff inside that made them human had taken a hike long ago and wasn't coming back. These were husks and nothing more.

When I reached the counter, I saw the fallen rack, the multicolored sea of cigarette packages, and underneath it all, a very pudgy, curly-haired zombie. She looked to be in her early twenties, and glasses with thick, black frames clung askew to her face. She saw me looking her way and struggled to free herself, rolling and rocking side to side.

I couldn't hold back a laugh and decided to give her a few minutes to recover while I shopped. I grabbed a yellow plastic shopping basket and loaded it up with energy shots, then added some beef jerky. I reached for the candy bars but remembered that awful photo showing off my rapidly expanding waistline and decided to pass on them. For now, anyway. I took a few jars of peanuts and some dried fruit, then topped off the basket with Funyuns because I remembered LaRon was a fan.

I returned to the checkout area and saw the cashier had freed herself from the tobacco avalanche and was almost back on her feet. I couldn't resist staring down her shirt as the deep valley of cleavage that revealed itself was almost hypnotizing.

"What a waste." I sighed, then forced myself to take my eyes off her pendulous breasts. In doing so, I saw a name tag reading, "Chelsea."

"Chelsea, huh?" She looked at me, and for a second, I thought maybe she recognized her name. Then I realized it was just the sound of my voice that had elicited the response. The way a dog tilts its head when you raise the pitch of your voice. That and her instinctual, insatiable desire to eat me. And not in the good way.

"We could've had fun, Chelsea."

She made it to her feet, then teetered, trying to get her balance as she stomped across a mound of cigarettes. I decided not to wait any longer and shoved the tip of the sword through the lens of her glasses. There was a light *pop* as her eyeball burst, and milky, pink-tinged goo ran out. After she fell, I wiped the blade of the sword against her shirt to cleanse it of the gore.

Before leaving the store, I spotted a display of instant lottery tickets, tore free a handful, and scratched them off one by one. They were all losers. Some things never changed.

WHEN I RETURNED to the garage, I found LaRon standing in the cargo area of the Jeep. He wore a welder's mask, and a cascade of sparks came down like orange rain. I knew enough to not look directly at the flame of the torch, so I mulled about the shop while LaRon worked.

The building was filled with a variety of tools and car parts. I sorted through it all, not knowing what most of it was and not really caring. I didn't know a carburetor from a catalytic converter. My vehicles had always been pieces of shit held together by duct tape and hope. When they conked out, I didn't bother getting them fixed. I just moved on to the next $250 Craigslist special.

Large pieces of sheet metal were stacked horizontally on a shelving unit. They were bright and shiny, almost mirror-like, and they caught my attention. When I brushed my hand against the edge, I opened a gash several inches long. Smooth move, dumbass.

I jerked my hand away, squeezing the wound closed while I looked for something to stop the bleeding. I found a box of cotton rags that looked unused and held one of them against the cut. Blood seeped through the white fabric, and I folded the rag over for extra absorption. That worked.

"The fuck you do?"

I turned and saw LaRon watching me. The welder's mask was tilted up, revealing his curious face. I held up my hand. "Cut myself."

"Good thing we're overrun with zombies and not vampires. Elsewise you'd bring all kinds of hell down on us." He paused, thinking. "Zombies can't smell blood, right?"

"I don't think so." Once upon a time, I didn't think they could climb stairs either, but I didn't mention that to him. I moved toward the Jeep, trying to see what the man was up to. I noticed a triangular frame had been welded onto the center of the Wrangler's roll bar.

"Help a brotha out," LaRon said.

I climbed into the back of the Jeep where LaRon had his hands under the Gatling Gun. Together, we crouched down and lifted.

"Careful now," LaRon said as he steered the gun toward the metal concoction he'd affixed to the roll bar. We set the gun on the triangle. "Hold it steady."

LaRon grabbed a wrench and made adjustments under the setup. He swore once, then stood, apparently satisfied. "You can let go now."

I thought the gun might topple off. I didn't see how LaRon's creation could be strong enough to keep it there, but when I let go, the Gatling Gun sat firmly atop the roll bar. LaRon grabbed the stock and swiveled it back and forth, flashing the grin that revealed his gold grills. "Not bad."

I had no great fondness for firearms, but even I had to admit this was impressive. "It's awesome, man. You know how to shoot it?"

"Hell yeah. Wouldn't of gone to this much trouble if I didn't. I know your white ass don't know nothing about guns."

"Guilty as charged." I knelt, examining LaRon's handiwork. The mount welded to the roll bar looked like it could withstand a tornado. "Where's you learn how to do this? Did you take metal shop in school or something?"

"Shit no. I learned this in the chop shop! Real-world experience."

As I considered my new friend's skills, I looked down at my sliced hand, then at the rows of sheet metal. "The doors come off Wranglers, don't they?"

LaRon nodded. "All you got to do is pop the pins. Why?"

"Are you up for another project?"

"Depends on the project."

Now it was my turn to smile.

IT TOOK LaRon all the afternoon and most of the evening to bring my idea to life, but when he was finished, we were both giddy with excitement.

The Jeep's doors were gone. In their place, LaRon had fabricated something akin to airplane wings which were five feet long, two feet deep and had razor-sharp edges.

LaRon showed me the mechanism he'd built off the Wrangler's original door hinges. Using that lever, the wings could be opened and locked in place with ease. Pulling it the other way retracted the wings and held them tight against the Jeep's body.

I thought it looked weird as shit, but exactly as I'd imagined it at the same time. Secretly, I wondered whether it would work in a real-world scenario, but in theory—my theory—it would be incredible.

"Let's try it out!" I couldn't wait.

LaRon raised his eyebrows. "Calm down, yo. I'm hungry and tired as fuck. We can play with our new toys tomorrow." He lit up a joint, and I knew the discussion was over.

I tried to calm myself. LaRon was right, after all. It was pitch black outside, and even with a Jeep armed with a machine gun and bladed wings, traveling at night was still a bad idea.

To get my mind off wreaking havoc, I grabbed the shopping bags I'd filled at the mini-mart, and we feasted. Soon after, as a food coma set in, we crashed on the floor.

JULY 31

I WOKE EARLY AND DOUBTED I'D SLEPT MORE THAN TWO HOURS. The excitement and curiosity were overwhelming. I allowed LaRon to sleep while I loaded the other guns, weapons, and supplies back into the Wrangler.

That took all of half an hour. When I was finished, I made sure to take extra hard footsteps as I walked, hoping LaRon would come awake. When that didn't work, I resorted to fake coughing.

After the fifth time, it worked. LaRon's eyelids fluttered, and he rolled onto his back, yawning as he looked at me. "What time is it? Oh dark thirty?"

"A little after seven, I think." I lied. I knew it was a quarter past six at the latest.

"Jesus, man. Can't you let a brother get his forty z's? We've got pretty much all the time in the world, in case you forgot."

"I know. I'm just anxious."

"You're always anxious. Why don't you smoke some of that weed?"

That wasn't a terrible idea, but I wanted to keep my head clear. "I can't. I'm driving, remember?"

"Ain't no one gonna bust you for driving under the influence." But LaRon worked his way into a sitting position. "What do we got left to eat?"

I tossed him an energy shot, hoping it would provide a nonverbal hint. LaRon scowled at me, but I thought he was simultaneously fighting off a grin.

"Whatever, yo. You wanna go, we'll go. Where's a good place around here to find a hella lotta people?"

I had just the spot in mind.

I LAID on the horn as I drove the Jeep into the parking lot of the local Walmart. There were a hundred or so cars but no zombies. I continued past them, only stopping when I reached the double glass doors.

"This should work," I said.

LaRon followed my gaze. The view inside was blocked by a smeary haze of zombies pressed against the glass. The ones up front had odd, flattened-out features as their bodies were smashed against automatic sliding doors, which were sealed shut in this powerless era. They clawed and scratched at the glass, their efforts fruitless.

"Want me to shoot it open?" LaRon asked, and I could hear the excitement in his voice. This was going to be crazy fun.

"I had another idea." I turned and fished through a duffle bag in the back seat, soon emerging with a grenade.

LaRon nodded in approval. "I like the way you think, Mead."

I pulled the pin and lobbed the grenade toward the doors. It hit the ground and rolled a few feet, ricocheting off the glass and coming to a stop as I hit the gas and sped away.

We only had to wait a moment before the explosion. I was surprised it wasn't louder. It sounded like a glorified cherry bomb—not the ground-shaking, earth-shattering results I'd expected—but it did the trick. The doors to the store shattered.

The ones up front took the brunt of the explosion. Shards of glass embedded themselves in their pale, gray skin, making them look a bit like ornate porcupines.

As we watched, one zombie's head was cleaved in two by a chunk of the metal door frame that whipped through the air like a propeller. Then, the soaring metal severed the arm of a store employee.

With the glass gone, the zombies emerged into the daylight, free and ready to feed. We had other plans, though. It was finally time to put our new toys to the test.

"Fire away," I told LaRon, who was all too eager to do just that. He slipped between the seats and into the rear of the Jeep. There, he took his position behind the Gatling Gun.

The zombies were maybe twenty yards from us, shuffling and stumbling. Easy targets. LaRon aimed the gun at them and took the crank in his right hand. But then he stopped and turned his attention to me.

"Ears." LaRon reached into the same bag from where I'd grabbed the grenade and pulled out two sets of protective earmuffs. He handed one to me and put on the other set.

Good thinking, I supposed, but at the same time, I wondered how this man from the projects of Baltimore knew so much about military weaponry and tactics. Hell, I'd grown up around guys who spent most of their lives in the woods, killing animals and shooting targets, but the thought of earplugs or headgear never would have occurred to me.

Before I could put any more thought into the matter, LaRon opened fire. Even wearing the earmuffs, the gun was shockingly loud. Much more impressive than the grenade. But even more awe-inspiring than the noise it made was the destruction the gun wrought.

Bullets ripped through the zombies at an almost impossibly fast pace. Their thick, clotted blood exploded through the air like back sleet. Several of the creatures' heads exploded, their decapitated bodies crashing to the ground, only to be replaced with a new front line.

LaRon kept shooting, and the zombies kept dying. From my spot in the driver's seat, I could feel heat coming off the gun like someone had set the oven to 500 degrees and left the door open. It was so hot I shrank sideways to try to get away from it.

Despite the heatwave, most of my attention remained on the horde as the gun tore them to pieces. Maybe guns aren't so bad after all, I thought. This weapon was certainly making quick work of the monsters, and, as I'd found out the hard way, I didn't know everything.

A pile of motionless zombies a few feet high littered the space in front of the store's entrance. I had no idea how many were dead but was sure it was dozens. Maybe a hundred. As amazing and wondrous as the experience was, I also wanted to put my own invention to use.

I turned to look at LaRon, whose arm kept cranking and firing the Gatling Gun. Speaking, or even shouting, over the roar of that weapon was impossible, so I grabbed the man's pants and gave a hard tug. LaRon stopped firing and turned his attention my way.

I mouthed, "Leave some for me."

LaRon nodded, pulled off the earmuffs, and tossed them into the bag. "Got a little carried away."

He couldn't stop grinning, and I didn't blame him one bit. At the same time, I was nervous. I expected the wings to work. There was no logical reason why they wouldn't. Yet how could they top the carnage of LaRon's gun? That was a proven war machine. The wings were something I'd dreamed up all on my own. I felt like an amateur musician going on stage to perform after AC/DC had just played a full set. Talk about performance anxiety.

As LaRon reclaimed the passenger seat, I drove the Jeep to the rear of the parking lot. We waited there as the zombies continued to flee the store. I hit the horn again to draw them our way, and it worked. I couldn't get an accurate count because my nerves were in overdrive, but I guessed there were still thirty or more.

Once they'd halved the distance between the store and the Jeep, I shifted the Wrangler back into drive, keeping my foot on the brake. I turned to LaRon and hoped I didn't look as nervous as I felt. "Ready?"

"Hell yeah. I was born ready. You got this shit, Mead."

I grabbed the lever and pulled it back. The wing on my side of the Jeep swung open, the metal glistening under the bright, mid-morning sun.

"Should I open mine too?" LaRon asked, his hand on the lever, ready.

"No. There's not really enough room in here. That'll work better on the highways." If it works at all, I thought.

I couldn't shake the memory of assuring Bundy that zombies couldn't climb stairs, only to be proven so very wrong. Bundy had never forgiven me, and that was also the end of our budding friendship. In a life where I'd so often been the punchline, I didn't want to go through that again. But it was far too late to turn back.

The zombies were thirty yards away now. The leader of the pack was a tall, pear-shaped woman in a yellow pantsuit and a white button-down. Or one that had been white many weeks ago. Now, the front of the shirt was stained red and brown and black like some sort of gory version of tie-dye. She reminded me a bit of Big Bird, and I stared at her undead face as I removed my foot from the brake and hit the gas.

The Wrangler lurched forward, slow off the start as usual but picking up speed as I kept putting more pressure on the pedal. Thirty yards became twenty. Ten.

I swerved to the right, so the zombies were no longer in front of the Wrangler but were instead in the path of the wing.

Five yards.

In my peripheral vision, I saw LaRon latch onto the grab handle on his side of the dash, steeling himself for what was to come. I knew I couldn't accept another failure, another embarrassment. I wanted to close my eyes but forced myself to watch. It was time.

Big Bird was still at the head of the flock, and that was bad news for her. The front edge of the wing caught her in the rib cage, and I felt the impact of the blow reverberate through the Jeep's body all the way to my hands on the steering wheel.

For a moment, I thought it wasn't working. That it wasn't sharp enough, and she was going to simply bounce backward. But that worry was gone in an instant when I witnessed her upper body toppling backward.

After her was an old man with so many age spots on his head that you could have played connect the dots. The wing sliced him in half at chest level, even severing both of his arms around the biceps.

The rest of the zombies were too close together for me to take in their features as the wing sliced them to pieces. Bursts of black blood and their dying groans filled the air as, one after another after another, they met their fate.

It was all over in seconds, and I hit the brakes so hard I threw myself forward, bouncing into the steering wheel, but I didn't even feel it because my system was so full of adrenaline. I made a hard U-turn, so fast that I almost fell out of the open door cavity, and made a mental note to wear my seat belt whenever the wing was extended from now on. And I had a feeling it was going to be getting a great deal of use.

Ahead of us, a bloody pile of zombies was strewn across the pavement. It looked like a mound of partially assembled mannequins, only these mannequins oozed blood and goo, and their spilled internal organs turned the parking lot black. And it looked incredible.

With no small effort, I forced myself to look away from the carnage I'd created and look to LaRon, who was bouncing up and down in his seat with excitement.

"Fucking shit, yo! That was epic! It was like a zombie blender! We've gotta do it again!"

I didn't know what made me happier, that this weapon I'd thought up actually worked—and worked so perfectly—or seeing the excitement on my friend's face.

I wanted to bask in the glory because it was such an oddly foreign feeling. I wished all the assholes who'd told me I'd never accomplish anything worthwhile in life were here to see this. Because the shit had hit the fan, and while most people were dead or dying, I was figuring out ways to not only survive but also to excel.

I realized another handful of zombies had emerged from the store. "Shoot em or dice em?" I asked LaRon.

"Dice the fuckers!"

I did just that.

WHEN ALL THE zombies were destroyed, we took turns posing in front of the bloodbaths we'd each created while the other took pictures. LaRon even got a sweet shot of me gripping the head and shoulders of a zombie that was still alive, even though the entire bottom part of its body was in a heap with the others.

Afterward, we raided Walmart, which was mostly free of the undead. I found three zombies inside and killed them with a sword, and LaRon shot two others, but overall it was an easier and more pleasant trip to the department store than any I'd experienced prior to the apocalypse.

While LaRon hit the sporting goods counter, filling a shopping cart to the brim with ammunition for the guns, I loaded another cart with food. Real food this time. Canned meat and vegetables, soup, dry goods. We had a long trip ahead of us, and even I knew that man could not survive on energy shots and snack cakes alone.

After getting enough food to last at least a week, I made my way to the office supply section, where I grabbed the thickest road atlas I could find. I searched until I found the small city of Bangor, then made a circle around the city, and, above it wrote, "Stephen King's house."

It looked almost impossibly far away, but what was life without adventure?

AUGUST 15

As a side effect of avoiding the cities and taking detours through the countryside, the road trip was slow and meandering. A week and a half in, and we'd only made it to western Connecticut. There, we settled in for the night in a sprawling green lodge on a lake that the signs declared "North Spectacle."

The view over the water, the mountains reflecting in the gently lapping waves, ended up being so pretty that we stayed for two days. I much enjoyed the break from the monotony of the road.

The cabin was well stocked, and I used the propane grill to boil some water and make spaghetti. I added some homemade sauce I'd found in the pantry, plenty of parmesan cheese, and tossed in handfuls of dried basil and parsley. I carried two plates of it onto the porch where LaRon had dozed off in a director's chair.

I cleared my throat, and he stirred. "Your dinner is served, Sir."

He sat up in the chair as I handed him a plate. He smiled as he took a whiff. "Damn boy, you got skills."

"I try."

I took a seat beside him, and we ate mostly in silence. It felt good to be cooking again, plus this was the first hot meal I'd had since the plague began. It surprised me how much I missed little things like that but not other people. I suppose I should have felt guilty about that, but I didn't.

LaRon finished his meal and licked the plate clean. "De-fuckin-licious. Now what's for dessert?"

He was joking, but I'd thrown together a boxed brownie mix which was baking on the grill. There were no eggs, of course, so I added extra oil and baking powder. I had no idea what the results would be, but it was worth a shot.

The brownies ended up on the flat side, and I had probably overdone it with the oil, but they were edible, and LaRon had no complaints. Well, almost none.

"Shoulda made these pot brownies."

"I'll remember that next time."

He grabbed a joint from behind his ear and lit it up. "No worries, my man. I always got a backup plan."

The sun had dipped toward the horizon, and the air was chilly. LaRon wrapped himself up in a blanket, but I didn't mind it.

"So, what's your end game, man? After we take this pilgrimage to Maine, I mean. What's next?"

I'd been thinking a lot lately. Now that I realized I had a future, I supposed I should do some planning. Chief on my mind was figuring out where to settle in for the long haul. I wasn't in any hurry to stop traveling but knew that, eventually, it would be the smart move.

I still felt West was the safest choice, but the more of the country I saw, the more I realized there were other options. Good options.

"I'm not sure. Don't you have an opinion?"

LaRon shrugged his shoulders. "Figured I'd scoot my ass back to Baltimore."

I was so surprised I think my mouth gaped open, and he noticed.

"Don't get me wrong. I'm having fun and all, but this home on the range shit ain't for me."

I was disappointed. More than disappointed. I was hurt. I

thought I'd found someone I could team up with for the long haul, but that idea now seemed foolish.

"But it's so dangerous there."

"There's danger everywhere, man. You don't get that yet? For all we know, that wood is full of bears or wolves or some shit. You could step outside to take a piss, and next thing you know, some mountain lion is using your dick for a chew toy."

"I'd rather take my chances with a random mountain lion than a million zombies."

"And that's where we're different. I ain't scared of the zombies. They slow as shit, and long as I don't do nothing stupid, they ain't gonna get me. They ain't hiding behind trees, waiting to pounce. They ain't cunning like that."

I guess he had a point there, but I fell silent. And unlike the silence over dinner, this one was awkward. Eventually, LaRon stood and stretched, yawning.

"Night, Mead. Don't get eaten out here."

I nodded as he disappeared into the lodge but gave no response. I didn't want to be alone again, and now, rather than focusing on keeping us safe, I realized I needed to keep LaRon interested. If he was enjoying himself, maybe he'd forget about Baltimore. About leaving me.

In the morning, we vacated the lodge.

AUGUST 19

THE MILES PASSED SLOWLY, AND WHILE I ENJOYED THE lackadaisical pace, I knew LaRon was bored. It had been five days since we'd killed a single zombie, and that was an elderly woman who might have weighed 90 pounds soaking wet and was about as dangerous as a kitten. It had been a week since we saw a cluster of the creatures large enough to warrant using the Gatling Gun.

To try to reinvigorate my friend's waning interest, I cut through the middle of Massachusetts and took a course that put us in Manchester, New Hampshire. My atlas and guidebook told me it was the largest city in northern New England, and, with a population of under a hundred thousand, it seemed like a place to find some excitement without taking too much of a risk.

It was a good choice. After we crossed the Merrimack River, we came upon a pileup on 293. Around the crashed cars and trucks was also a cluster of zombies fifteen deep. I glanced at LaRon and saw him grinning, a rare sight in recent days.

"You want to get 'em?"

LaRon jumped up. "Hell yeah!" He squirmed into the back seat and took his place behind the Gatling Gun. I threw on the earmuffs, and it was just in time because LaRon was raring to go.

A zombie in a three-piece suit was closest to us, and I got a good look at him as his head blew apart. Chunks of destroyed skulls flew through the air, and a piece that still contained shards of the zombie's wispy gray hair embedded itself in the face of a chunky teenage boy in a Manchester Monarchs jersey.

The fan had no chance to react because he was next in the line of fire, and his pudgy face imploded. It was less than thirty seconds after LaRon had killed all of them, but the sound made by the gun was like a canon on the otherwise noiseless afternoon, and I could see more zombies approaching in the distance. Twenty or more, at least, but they were only ants at the far distance. I drove around the crashed vehicles, then decided to wait and watch.

"There's a few coming in from behind," LaRon said as he grabbed an AK-47. "I need to stretch my legs anyway."

He was gone before I could respond. I thought leaving the Jeep was unwise. It was like abandoning your castle while under siege, but I wasn't in charge and had no call to issue orders. Instead, I leaned across the passenger seat and opened the wing on that side, then I did the same on my own. As the AK went off behind me, its rat-a-tat-tat sound filling the air, I drove forward.

I was a good quarter mile from the incoming zombies. By the time I reached them, the Jeep was closing in on forty miles an hour. The zombies crowded the roadway from one side to the other, and they were packed in tight. I didn't even bother trying to get a head count.

The push bar on the front of the Jeep made first contact. A short female zombie with jet-black hair absorbed the brunt of the impact with her face. I winced as I heard her bones break and powered forward. The Wrangler bounced as it rolled over her body, and then the wings went to work at the sides of the vehicle.

The creatures growled and gasped, but their sounds were drowned out by the wet, thick noises that resulted from their bodies being sliced and severed. I watched as decapitated heads and severed arms flew as topless bodies collapsed to the ground.

One beefy arm with a tribal tattoo soared past the driver's side door. The windshield became so heavily coated with blood that I needed to turn on the wipers and hit the washer fluid to see through the carnage. Black blood rained down on me.

By the time I'd rammed my way through the crowd and emerged on the other side, I was coated with a fine mist of coagulated gore. Almost frantic, I wiped it from my face on the chance that whatever the undead bastards had was catching. My zombie knowledge, gleaned from decades of horror films, told me that was possible. Most times, a person could only be infected by a bite, but other bodily fluids sometimes did the trick, and I wasn't about to let myself come down with a bad case of zombie-itis. I poured a bottle of water over my face and washed as well as possible.

After cleansing myself, I made a U-turn on the highway, trying to avoid the dismembered bodies that covered the road on the off chance that a shattered bone might puncture one of the Wrangler's tires, then returned to the approximate spot where LaRon and I had parted ways.

He sat on the concrete median, rifle in hand, and unable to hold back a broad grin.

"What are you so happy about?"

LaRon stood and moved to the Jeep. "I feel like fucking Rambo, man. I ain't never had this much fun."

I knew the feeling. The adrenaline rush achieved by wiping out massive amounts of the undead was high far more intoxicating than weed. Maybe he would grow to love life on the road after all.

AUGUST 24

WE TOOK SIDE ROADS UP THE COAST, PASSING THROUGH LITTLE towns like Ogunquit, Bath, and Rockport on our way to Bangor. As stunned as I was to see the ocean for the first time in Maryland, the Maine coastline almost overwhelmed me with its beauty. The coastline was more rock than sand, more pine trees than boardwalks. I didn't say anything to LaRon then, but I felt like I could call this place home.

The days were long in the summer, and by nine at night, there was still enough light to see. The golden glow of the setting sun off the ocean was irresistible, and we decided to stop in Moose Point State Park and photograph the sunset.

The only downside was the bugs. Why in the hell hadn't the plague done something about the bugs? They were dining on LaRon like he was a smorgasbord, and I wasn't faring much better.

"We need some of that DEET shit," LaRon said as he smashed a bloodsucker against his forearm.

"Doesn't that cause seizures or something?"

"Hell, man, I'd welcome a seizure right about now. Better than itching myself to death." He dug his fingernails into his skin, scratching away. "These are worse than the damn sand flies in the desert."

"Desert?" Another surprise.

LaRon half-smiled. "Yeah, man. I'm a world fuckin traveler. Courtesy of my favorite uncle. Sam."

The pieces finally came together in my head, albeit a little slower than I care to admit. "You were in the military?"

LaRon gave a barely perceptible nod. "Army. Did my four years active duty. Still had a couple to go in the reserves when this shit went down."

"I never would have guessed." Incredulity filled my voice, and I immediately wished I could take the remark back.

"Why? Because I'm a gangster?"

"No. I didn't mean it that way. I just... I thought."

LaRon grabbed a small rock from the ground beside him and chucked it my way. It bounced off my shoulder. "Like I told you before, I was an entrepreneur. I wasn't ever in no gang. I guess I was what you'd call an independent contractor.

"Anyway, the Army was my ma's idea. Thought it would keep me off the streets. So instead of getting shot at in drive-bys, I got to dodge bullets and bombs in Iraq. You know that saying, 'Mother knows best'? Shit man, not my ma. She almost got my black ass blown to bits."

"It was that bad?"

"Not always. Not even most of the time. But when it was bad, it was pretty damn terrible. And I wasn't joking about getting my ass blown up. I meant it in the literal sense."

He jumped to his feet and, without a warning or an ounce of shame, dropped his pants and boxers. "See."

I didn't want to look but felt obligated since I'd brought it up. A glistening, black scar snaked its way from his ass cheek, around his pelvis, and halfway down his thigh. My eyes must have grown wide when I took it in because LaRon used both his hands to cover his substantial penis, which had been swinging free and clear up until that point.

"Now don't you be looking at my dick and getting no jungle fever. I like you and all, Mead, but you ain't my type."

My head snapped away so fast I strained my neck, and LaRon burst out laughing. "You're too fuckin easy." He pulled up his pants.

I could feel the heat in my face and knew I must be beet red. I wanted to change the subject, or at least bring it back around to where we'd started. "So, what happened?"

"We were out on patrol, just doing a routine sweep. Guy ten yards from me stepped on an IED. I caught some shrapnel."

"What happened to him?"

LaRon grimaced. "Put it this way, I was the lucky one."

"Ouch."

"Yeah."

"I don't know how you did it. Go over there and put your life on the line for what, twenty grand a year?"

"I didn't do it for the money, man. I did it for our country."

"The country?"

"Hell yeah."

"What did this country ever do for you?"

"It ain't about that. It's doing the right thing. Putting other people's needs first. The greater good and all that shit. Ain't that the point?"

I wondered if he really believed that. I'd never put anyone ahead of myself. I never saw the point because I'd never met anyone who deserved it.

"I'm not exactly the heroic type."

"You don't know that. I got faith in you, Mead."

For whatever reason, that made me feel good. And maybe he was right.

LaRon smacked another black fly that had taken up residence on his chest. "That Stephen King house better be goddamn amazing to put up with this shit." He wrapped his sleeping bag around himself, trying to conceal as much exposed skin as possible. "You wake me up when it's time to hit the road."

"I will." I watched him zipper the bag closed, completely sealing himself off against the biting insects. Despite their annoying presence, I wasn't ready to go to sleep. I listened to the waves break against the rocky shoreline and imagined myself doing something important, something heroic, for once in my life.

AUGUST 25

WE ROLLED INTO BANGOR AROUND NOON. THE TOWN HAD A typical amount of zombies. Not enough to bother breaking out the wings or the Gatling Gun. I ran down the ones in the roadway, and we mostly ignored those roaming the sidewalks or stumbling through lawns.

Every now and then, LaRon would line one up in the sights of whatever pistol he'd decided to carry that day and plink them in a way that reminded me of a sideshow shooting booth, only there was no fat, sketchy carny there to hand him a prize when they fell.

I barely noticed the monsters because I was on the lookout for the sprawling, red Victorian mansion I'd gazed at so often online. I remembered the street name but not the house number, but it turned out that it didn't matter.

The streets were almost too quaint. Every house was old but immaculate. Trees bursting with lush summer foliage lined the road and crowded the sidewalks. The only clue that something was amiss was the unkept lawns with almost knee-high grass growing wild and out of control.

My head pivoted on my neck like I was watching a tennis match, side to side, back and forth, as I sought out the house of the man whose every book I'd devoured ever since reading Salem's Lot in the fifth grade. And as we made it halfway down the street, I found it.

Lining the front edge of the property was a black wrought iron fence that looked ordinary enough at first glance but, upon closer inspection, featured bats and spiderwebs and creatures that looked like a mix between dragons and gargoyles. It was like Stephen King had paired up with a blacksmith and said, "They drove all the way to fucking Bangor for this. Let's give 'em something to see!" And part of me thought he'd said it exactly like that.

I stared at that house the way I'd imagine a religious person does when seeing some great Holy building or artifact. Or maybe like a groom when he sees his soon-to-be bride standing at the end of the aisle. I didn't know if I was in awe or love or shock or all three at once. I couldn't even get a word out. I just stared.

LaRon, however, was not so tongue-tied. "Baller had a big ass house!"

His words broke my concentration, my daze. "Huh? Yeah."

"So, what you waiting for?"

"What do you mean?"

"Pictures, man. We didn't come up here to go away with nothing but memories." He pointed at the front gate. "Get yo ass over there and pose like a motherfucker."

I did just that as he snapped away. In some photos, I smiled and pointed. In others, I pretended to be impaled on the gate. In others, I got down on my knees and worshipped the house of the man who'd had a bigger impact on my life than my own parents.

I doubt I ever would have grown weary of the fun, but the photo shoot was interrupted when LaRon looked past me. "Uh. Mead?"

"What?"

"Is that..." He didn't finish the question. He just pointed.

I turned to follow his gesture, peering through the gate, past the bushes and shrubbery that framed the property. And then I saw what he saw, and my heart almost burst.

Stephen King, or the zombie that used to be Stephen King, stumbled past a white Mercedes parked beside the house and into the driveway. It, or he, was coming toward us.

"Oh shit. Oh damn. Oh fuck. Oh shit." It was like I'd lost my entire vocabulary aside from vulgarities and 'ohs'.

He was tall and lean and wore a blue chambray shirt and jeans, and he looked just like he had in interviews and cameos in movie adaptations of his books. Aside from the fact that he was a zombie. Even his glasses still clung to his face.

"Oh shit," I repeated.

"You said that already."

I'd almost forgotten LaRon was there. I looked away from zombie Stephen King to my friend. "It's Stephen King."

"I know that. I ain't been living under a rock all my life."

"It's Stephen King. For real."

"But he's dead, yo."

"I don't even care."

Throughout this journey, I hadn't dared allow myself to imagine that King would actually be here, alive or dead. To hope for such a possibility would have been setting myself up for disappointment. But he was here after all.

He was only a few yards away at that point. I could see that he was thinner than usual, almost frail. Unlike many of the zombies, he didn't have dried blood on his face. No chunks of masticated flesh stuck in his teeth. You poor guy, I thought. Probably haven't had anything to eat in weeks.

A part of me, a bigger part than I should probably admit, thought I should sacrifice myself to him. To let Stephen King eat me. That would have been the most perfect death of all time.

But as he got closer, my survival instinct kicked back in, and I realized, as epic as that might have been, I preferred to stay alive.

I did, however, have another idea. "Get the camera ready," I said to LaRon.

"What the fuck you gonna do?"

"Just do it."

"Cracker thinks he's Nike now," LaRon muttered as I crossed the short distance between zombie Stephen King and myself. A yard away. A foot.

Then, I grabbed him around the waist with my right arm and pulled him in close to me. I looked to LaRon, who stared bug-eyed.

"Take the picture!"

Zombie Stephen King was not amused by my antics and, being a good eight or nine inches taller than me, thrashed his upper body, trying to break free, but I held on tight.

LaRon raised the camera and clicked.

"Another one!"

That time, I grinned and flashed a thumbs up. LaRon snapped another shot, and I heard him laugh. He was getting into it now.

"Act like he's gonna bite you!" he said.

I repositioned myself, letting go of King and backing half a yard away. I pretended to cower, holding my arms in front of my face as if to shield myself and heard the camera click again.

"Let me get in on this!" LaRon ran toward us. "Hold him."

I did. I was on King's right side, and LaRon sidled up on the left. He held the camera out in front and above us, as far as his arm could reach. "Selfie time!"

We both cheesed it up, then LaRon flipped the camera over to check the shot. "Oh damn, that's a good one!"

I looked too, even though I could feel King struggling between us, trying to break free, trying to attack. The photo was indeed a good one. Better than good. It was perfect. Even Stephen King had looked at the camera for the shot.

We carried on like that for twenty minutes of more taking turns posing with him, getting pictures of King alone. It was morbid as hell, but also maybe the greatest moment of my entire life. Scratch the maybe. It was the best.

Zombie Stephen King grew more furious the longer we goofed, and I eventually started to feel a little guilty. All the poor guy wanted was a hot meal. And even if that hot meal of choice was human flesh, he was only doing what came naturally. I couldn't blame him.

"All right," I said to LaRon. "We should probably stop."

"Okay, man. It's your call. Should I grab one of your swords for ya, or do you want me to finish him?" His free hand dropped to the butt of the pistol tucked in his waistband.

Before I could stop myself, I smacked his hand away from the gun.

"What the hell, man?" His face was confused, and I thought I saw some anger mixed in.

"I'm sorry. I didn't mean to. But Jesus, LaRon. We can't kill Stephen King."

LaRon raised his eyebrow. "He's already dead, Mead. He's a zombie."

"I know." I looked back to King, who had become tangled up in a rhododendron bush, snarling and growling as he tried in vain to free himself. "It's just that I can't. We can't."

I thought he might punch me. Or maybe pull out the gun anyway and blow away Stephen King. It would have been the smart thing to do, after all. And if he'd been some random zombie, I'd have done it myself.

I risked a glance at LaRon and saw his hands at his sides, not on the gun. Not balled up in fists. And there was even a smile on his face. "Yo man, I get it. But what are we gonna do with him?"

It was my turn to smile, and I glanced at the Jeep.

LaRon must have read my mind. "Aw, hell no. We ain't taking him with us."

He was right, of course. Even if he was Stephen King, we couldn't bring a zombie along on our adventures, unless we wanted to die.

As I ushered Stephen King into his house, he thrashed and clawed at me. I got him through the door, and he stumbled, falling onto the oak floor.

"Sorry about that, Mr. King. But you need to stay inside where it's safe."

He growled as he awkwardly climbed back to his feet.

"And I know you heard this all the time, but I just have to say it. You scared the shit out of me."

SEPTEMBER 2

AFTER LEAVING BANGOR BEHIND, WE TOOLED AROUND MAINE but found a whole lot of nothingness in the center of the state and eventually turned south again. We ended up in Portland so that LaRon could get his zombie-killing fix.

I watched, amused, as he used the Gatling Gun for so long that I could see the exertion had physically exhausted him. Well, part of it was the exertion. The other was the fact that he'd been hitting the marijuana hard all morning long, and his eyes were so bloodshot they looked like they might spontaneously bleed.

"How about we take a break?" I suggested.

He pretended he wasn't winded. "If you say so."

"I do."

Relief washed over his face as he resumed his usual spot in the passenger seat. Out of the corner of my eye, I could see his chest rising and falling rapid fire.

"What was that? Seventy-five?" I asked.

"Shit, man, a hundred and ten at a bare minimum. You need to work on your counting," he said with a grin.

"What can I say, you're just too damned fast?"

As I drove, he dug through a duffle bag. "Everything okay?"

"We're getting low on ammo. Real damn low. You see a gun shop, you best pull in."

It didn't take more than half an hour of driving aimlessly before we came across a sign for Abe's Ammo. Turning into the parking lot, we saw Abe's was the largest store in a shopping plaza that contained a handful of other businesses, a gas station, and two fast food restaurants. Abe's itself featured a rambling storefront painted camo green, brown, and black.

"Will this do?"

LaRon nodded. "This state ain't all bad."

What was bad was that a few hundred zombies had made the plaza's parking lot their home. And there were just enough cars parked haphazardly throughout the area that the Jeep's bladed wings couldn't be extended and were useless.

"Do you have enough bullets to take care of this?"

LaRon shook his head. "Not even close. Shit!"

"Don't worry about it. We'll find somewhere else." I started to turn the Jeep back to the exit but felt LaRon grab my arm.

"Naw, man. I got an idea."

I looked at him and saw him staring off to the side. Following his gaze, I realized he was looking at the gas station. "We've got plenty of gas."

"I know that. I don't want to get gas for the Jeep. I want to use it on them."

I still wasn't sure what he meant, but when he pointed to the side of the gas station, it started making sense. Parked at the back corner of the building was a fuel truck. Its silver tanker blazed almost white under the midday sun.

"You aren't thinking..."

LaRon smiled, blissful and high. "We're gonna light these bitches up."

I ran down four zombies which loitered around the gas station, keeping the RPMs low and the engine as quiet as possible, so we didn't draw the attention of the hundreds of others who meandered about the parking lot.

The coast was clear as we parked beside the massive tanker. LaRon wasted no time before jumping out of the Wrangler and jogging to the rear of the truck.

I followed and watched as he pulled a hose as thick as my thigh from the truck. He quickly connected it to a valve. I'm sure I could have figured out how all of this worked on my own, given enough time, but LaRon seemed too familiar to be learning on the fly.

"Is there anything you can't do?"

"I can't dance for shit." He glanced up at me. "You learn to do a little bit of everything in the Army. You think your Jeep's thirsty? Try keeping a fleet of Humvees running day in day out." He took a deep drag off a joint.

"Think that's smart?"

He stared at me, confused, and I mimed smoking. "You think I'm gonna blow us up?"

"Maybe."

"That shit only happens in movies." But he pinched the joint off and dropped it into his pocket. He finished connecting the hose and pointed to a lever above where it connected to the tanker. "That's your shut-off valve. Soon as you open that, fuel's gonna come out about a hundred gallons a minute."

"Why are you telling me this?"

"Because you're manning the hose."

"Me?" I didn't like this plan.

"Can you drive the truck?"

He had me there.

"I'll circle through the lot, and you douse the bitches. Once we're finished, you shut the valve and meet me at the front of the truck."

"And then what?"

LaRon only grinned. He hopped into the cab, and I had no opportunity to protest. This was his show, and it had begun.

I held onto the hose and jogged close behind the truck as he drove toward the zombies. The weight of the hose was shocking, and by the time we were amid them, I was already out of breath. This plan got worse with every passing second.

The brakes shrieked as LaRon stopped the truck, and if any zombie in the area hadn't been aware of our presence before then, that sound beckoned them like a homing beacon.

The creatures shuffled toward us, growling and snarling. The scent of their death cologne on that hot day sickened me. The closest were a few yards away, and I knew it was time to act. I grabbed the lever and tried to turn it. Only it didn't budge.

I tried again. Nothing. "Oh fuck!"

I looked behind me, and a half dozen zombies were within feet of it. All my weapons were in the Jeep, and I had a feeling I was screwed. My only thought was that I could dive under the truck and find some axle or part to hold onto while LaRon drove me to safety, but the realistic part of my brain knew I wasn't strong enough to hang on for more than a few seconds.

With no other options, I tried the lever one more time, jerking down on it with all my body weight. And finally, that time, it turned.

The hose went rigid, and gasoline shot out of the end, soaking the ground. I ran to it and picked it up, no easy task, then aimed it at the zombies like a fireman trying to snuff out flames.

The fuel soaked them, and the creatures stumbled backward. Several, knocked off balance by the force of the flow, fell to the pavement. I doused every zombie close enough to reach with the hose, then glanced at the cab where LaRon watched. I gave him a thumb's up, and he drove again.

We repeated this stop, spray, and go act seven times. It took nearly fifteen minutes, but eventually, all the zombies had received their baptism by gasoline, and I closed the lever, which was much easier than opening it.

I ran to the cab and climbed inside, and LaRon drove us away from the zombies.

"You stink, man."

The smell of petroleum filled my nose and had apparently also permeated my clothing. Maybe even my pores. "Sorry."

"You should be."

"Now what?"

He parked at the mini-mart. I grabbed a spear from the Jeep, but LaRon didn't take any weapons.

"Don't you want a gun or something?"

"Naw, man. I'm good." He reached into his pocket and, from it, pulled a lighter. "This." He took one of the red plastic jugs of gasoline from the Wrangler. "And this is all we're gonna need. You'll see."

I watched as LaRon strolled toward the zombies, many of which were coming our way. I was amazed at his nonchalant attitude and wondered how much of it was genuine bravery and how much was the constant marijuana fog.

He opened the nozzle on the gas can and poured a trail of fuel along the pavement, stopping when he was a few yards from the nearest zombies. Then, he set the can on its side and returned to me.

"Sit back and enjoy the show, Mead." He watched them come, and when the creatures reached the can, LaRon knelt at the beginning of the gas trail, flicked his lighter, and lit the fuel on fire.

Flames raced up the path and reached the gas can within a second. The fire hit the can, and it exploded with a small *whoosh*. The flames leaped into the air and lit a zombie in a yellow rain slicker on fire.

The monster awkwardly spun and twirled as first its clothing and then its body burned. It bumped into a tall, almost skeletal man in a plaid shirt, then collided with a woman in a cute kitten sweatshirt. At his touch, those two also caught on fire.

LaRon's plan was indeed solid, and it was coming together at breakneck speed. One after another after another, the zombies were set ablaze. Less than two minutes later, it seemed like the entire parking lot was a massive, raging inferno.

LaRon bounced on his feet, as excited as a kid who just saw Santa Claus live and in person for the very first time. He grabbed the camera from his pocket and snapped some photos, then tossed it to me.

"Gotta make a Kodak fucking moment outta this."

He posed in front of the burning zombies, grinning, flexing, pointing, giving, giving the peace sign. This was his moment in the sun, but as the fire grew behind him, I realized that moment might be short-lived.

"It won't be long before the whole block goes up," I said.

He glanced back and nodded. "We better get our asses lootin'!"

We ran to Abe's Ammo, making a wide circle around the fiery mass of zombies. The plate glass window at the front of the store was shattered, giving us easy access. Although it was partially burglarized, there was still plenty for the taking.

To me, though, everything in the store might as well have been from another planet. "What am I supposed to look for?"

"The Gatling Gun takes 50 caliber. We need a bunch of other shit, but you'll never remember all the numbers, so focus on 50s. I'll check here, you look in the storeroom."

That sounded good to me. I headed into the back, where there must have been fifteen metal storage racks, each filled with boxes and standing taller than me. Fortunately, the boxes were numbered, and I began scanning for something indicating 50 caliber ammo.

I was nine rows deep when I found it. There were twenty cases or more. I grabbed one off the shelf, excited to show my friend this prize.

"Guess what I found?"

I moved toward the storefront but only made it halfway there when I heard a muffled thud.

"LaRon?" There was no response. I waited. Listened. "LaRon? Everything okay bout there?"

I hear another thud. Then, LaRon's voice. "Get away from me, you fucking Freddy Krueger bitch!"

I tossed down the box and grabbed my spear as I ran toward his voice. Before I got there, I heard something between a scream and a gasp.

I ran into the store, conduit spear in hand and ready to battle, only to see LaRon standing atop one of the display cases, surrounded by more than twenty zombies, all of which were on fire. The flames had set the store ablaze too. The carpet burned like dry grass, and flames licked at the walls. At anything that was flammable.

The sight of it overwhelmed me. I stared, too shocked to move. To fight. To help.

One of the fire zombies grabbed onto LaRon's pant leg, and he kicked it away. Then he kicked it again in the head, and it stumbled backward a step, but other zombies immediately took its place.

I looked past them and saw all the zombies from the parking lot, the hundreds of burning zombies, marching in our direction. Dozens were at the front of the store, pushing their way inside, and a flaming sea followed.

LaRon's shoelaces were ablaze, and he kicked his feet, trying to put it out, but the flames only spread, claiming his shoes, then licking at his pants. All the while, more and more burning zombies packed in around him.

It looked like he was standing on an atoll in the middle of a fiery ocean. Arms reached for him. Hands clawed at him. The flames spread up his pant legs, toward his midsection. That's when he started to scream.

My mind raced. What could I do? How could I possibly get in there and save him? No matter how many scenarios I ran through my mind, they all ended the same way. With both of us dying.

The flames had reached the ceiling, and the cheap tile lit up like tinder. The entire store was burning, floor, walls, and ceiling. And the oasis in the middle was LaRon on the display case, fighting for his life. And losing.

Then, he saw me. He'd been flailing wildly, fighting against the flames, and his body turned in my direction. Before I could react, our eyes met. I saw a measure of relief in his face. Some hope clawing through the pain.

"My goose is good as cooked, man," he said, and it was as if the zombies realized he was speaking to someone. A third of the horde turned my way and staggered toward me, bringing the fire with them.

I knew there was no way to rescue him and be the hero. There were too many zombies. Too many flames. And no time. Stepping so much as a single foot into that store would have meant death for both of us.

"I'm sorry." I doubted my voice carried over the roar of the fire and the hungry groans of the zombies, but he seemed to understand.

"It's aight." He gave a slight tip of his head as the flames licked his face.

Then, I ran the other way.

I fled through the rear exit. Because all the zombies were focused on getting into the store where LaRon was either being eaten or burned alive or both, I had no problem sprinting to the Jeep unnoticed. It wasn't until I got behind the wheel that I dared look back at Abe's Ammo. I half expected to see LaRon, an undead, burning version of him, emerging from the store like a wraith, coming for me, eager to seek his vengeance.

All I saw was the entire store ablaze. The fire had spread to the surrounding businesses, and the whole row was going up in flames. Black smoke billowed into the air, the smoke so thick it drowned out the midday sun.

It was over.

NOVEMBER 29

I haven't felt like writing much. In the weeks after LaRon's death, I meandered around Maine and even ventured into Canada for a spell. I took my own personal tour of Acadia National Park, dined dockside in Bar Harbor, and ended up at a rundown lodge on the coast where the scenery was beautiful and there wasn't a zombie in sight.

It was a good life, a far better one than I deserved. The land was beautiful and bountiful. Wild strawberries and blueberries helped satiate my sweet tooth as I went cold turkey off junk food. I even managed to become an adequate fisherman. It seemed like the marine life had been spared in the apocalypse, and with a rod and reel, I caught a few a week. I even bagged a couple lobsters, and let me say, everything I'd ever heard about Maine lobsters was true. All of that, coupled with canned goods, kept my belly full enough.

I made a point to exercise, going for daily jogs around the property to burn calories and melt away some of the spare tire I'd grown. For muscle tone, I went to work with my axe, only I wasn't killing zombies. Now, I was chopping wood. I wasn't a bodybuilder by any means, but I thought my arms felt a little harder. I needed to do anything I could to stay in shape because, as I'd learned the hard way, you never knew when you might need to fight your way out of trouble.

Through the months, I saw several deer, two moose, and even a black bear which lumbered across the lawn one morning while I was outside gutting a fish. And believe me, it's not just bears that shit in the woods.

The lodge had an old rifle, but I didn't know if it worked. Even if it did, I couldn't have shot any of them. This was their home as much as it was mine. Hell, it was more theirs. I was nothing more than an interloper. A chickenshit interloper at that. I wasn't any more deserving of living than they were. Maybe I was even less.

It was lonely at times, but worse than the solitude was having to relive the last few months over and over again. I didn't know how many other survivors remained in the world, but I thought they were probably better off with me in the middle of nowhere in Maine, far away from them. After all, everyone I teamed up with died, and there was already plenty of death to go around without me speeding up the process.

Living out the rest of my days alone seemed a fitting solution all the way around. Besides, I liked it here. Even the bugs weren't bad as summer gave way to fall.

I made the lodge my home until early November. The fall foliage provided a breathtaking backdrop, like something out of one of those paintings the guy with the curly hair did on public access TV. But fall in Maine wasn't like fall in Pennsylvania, and when the leaves came down, they were replaced with frigid winds that cut like saw blades into my bones.

The old lodge wasn't insulated, and the wood-burning fireplace did little to keep the cold at bay. One morning, I woke up with my eyelids frozen shut. I had to pry them open and lost pretty near all my eyelashes in the process. I knew that if I'd slept a little later or waited too much longer, I would have ended up a Mead-cicle. By the time I'd have thawed out, come springtime, I'd be just another zombie. I hated to admit it, to accept it, but I couldn't survive a winter there.

I'D WAITED TOO long to flee. Maybe it wasn't winter by the calendar, but it was winter as far as the weather was concerned. Between blizzards and whiteouts and snowdrifts so deep I couldn't tell whether I was even on a road anymore, it took me a week to escape Maine. And the situation was slow to improve, even as I headed south.

My beloved Jeep was betraying me. When I secured the vehicle, I'd given little thought to the downside of having no roof and, later, no doors. Now, with snow and ice and wind hammering away at me through the openings, I thought death might be imminent.

Somewhere in Massachusetts, I found a clothing outlet store. Everything on the racks were summer styles, but the backroom yielded an insulated parka. It was two sizes too big, but that was fine. I looked a bit like the marshmallow man, and my movement was severely limited, but it was a worthwhile tradeoff because I could drive the Jeep without feeling like my nipples were going to slice through my denim shirt.

It was almost December before I reached Pennsylvania. It was like winter there too, and snow covered the ground and roads, but at least the constant Nor'easter I'd been driving through was over. These were driving conditions I was used to, and even though the going was slow, I could make steady progress.

I was driving through the Wilds, a remote north-central part of the state which was little more than trees and elk, so I was pretty damn flabbergasted when I saw a few dozen zombies on the road. It was more zombies clumped together in one place than I'd seen in months. Since LaRon's fiery demise. But I tried not to think about that.

The creatures crowded the roadway, filling it from one side to the other. They were moving away from me, and I considered plowing through the middle of them, but the snow was a foot and a half deep, and I worried that I'd wreck.

I hadn't used the Wrangler's wings in months and half expected them to be frozen and unmovable, but I decided to try anyway. It took about all the strength I possessed, but I first opened the wing on my side, then the passenger. I idled there for a minute, steeling myself for the coming carnage.

Since that day at the shopping center, I hadn't killed a single zombie, and I didn't miss it in the slightest, but seeing the monsters shambling along the snow-covered road stirred something inside me. They reminded me of my purpose. I might not be good at keeping other people alive, but I was good at killing zombies. Damn good.

I eased down the gas pedal, not wanting to floor it and spin out. My speed built gradually. Ten miles per hour. Twenty. Thirty. I didn't risk going any faster in the snow.

I was half a mile from the creatures and closing fast. I wondered why they were all there. This section of Pennsylvania wasn't as remote as Maine, but it was damn close. What's your deal, I wondered.

Their deal didn't matter, though, because they were about to die. Or die again. When I was ten yards away, the zombies at the back of the pack turned to me. Their skin had gone almost white in the cold, which made their gray eyes stand out even more.

The first in line was a woman in a knock-off Pittsburgh Pirates jersey, the kind with the plastic iron-on letters and numbers. She snarled as my vehicle rushed toward her.

"Time to die."

The wing on the passenger side ripped through her torso, splitting the jersey's numbers in half. After that, it all happened so fast that I didn't bother trying to differentiate them. One after another, they were either chopped or diced by the wings, or I rammed into them with the bumper and drove over them.

The Jeep bounced and shuddered like I was driving down a

rock path, the kind they always showed in Wrangler commercials about having the freedom to drive anywhere. I thought they should make a commercial showing what else the Jeeps were capable of doing.

I glanced in the rearview mirror and saw a trail of gore staining the otherwise pristine, white snow. It looked like a red river. And it made me smile. I hadn't done much smiling in a while, and it felt off but good.

I realized the steady thudding impact of the Jeep and the wings hitting zombies had ceased, and I returned my gaze to the road ahead of me. At first, I thought the path was clear, but then I spotted what looked like a brownish-gray wig. That didn't make sense, though. I assumed it must be an animal of some sort. Maybe an oversized groundhog or wolverine.

I hit the brakes, slowing as fast as possible without risking going into a skid. I wondered if the zombies had been chasing this thing. Following it in hopes of a warm meal.

I was only yards away when I realized this wasn't an animal pelt. It was a mop of hair. Human hair. And underneath it was a body sprawled out on the snow-covered road.

After months of living through the plague and apocalypse, my first thought was that this was another zombie. I had ceased expecting to find a living human being, and the reasonable part of my mind told me to run over it and get out of there. This was all just a little too weird.

But the curious part of my mind wanted—needed—to see what the hell was going on. And besides, if this was a zombie, it wouldn't be a challenge to destroy. I grabbed one of the metal conduit spears from the back seat and slipped out of the Wrangler.

I had to walk around the wing, which meant I had to step off the road and shimmy down a small ditch. I felt ice water seep into my boots and said a few swear words because I knew it was going to be a long time before they dried out and my feet warmed up.

Once around the wing, I clambered out of the ditch and back

onto the road, stomping my feet as if that would do any good. Numbness was already setting in.

I was close enough to the thing in the road to reach it with the spear, so I extended it, trying to be as careful as possible. I slipped the spear under the thing's hair and lifted. That did no good because the zombie or man or whatever had decided to take a siesta in the middle of the road was face down.

"Damn it."

I took a few more steps toward it, circling, trying to get a better look. I realized that this figure wasn't totally naked but damn close. I could see tufts of wiry hair sprouting from its back, then a pair of briefs that blended in perfectly with the snow, then two thick, muscular, and hairy legs ending in bare feet.

"Jesus Christ."

The feet looked like beef run through a meat grinder. The soles were ragged, so much so that even at a distance of eight feet, I could see where the flesh was ripped and torn away. I supposed they should have been bleeding, but they were most likely frozen.

I poked the torso with the end of the spear. Nothing happened. I poked again, harder. Hard enough to draw blood.

It took a moment, in the cold, but blood did escape the small puncture wound. Red blood. Human blood.

I dropped the spear and ran to the man's side, dropping to my knees in the snow. I grabbed him by the shoulder and rolled him. He flipped over with a grunt.

His face was as hairy as the back of his head. A patchy, multicolored beard obscured most of his features, but I could see his eyes. They were closed.

"Hey, buddy. Wake up for me." I gave him a shake. "Wake up, and I'll get you out of here."

His eyelids fluttered but didn't open. I saw that his beard was caked in frozen snot and drool and chunks of what looked like blood.

"What the fuck happened to you, man?"

He didn't answer. I grabbed him under his arms and tried to lift him into a sitting position, but he was a big dude, probably a foot taller than me and half again my weight, and I only succeeded in dragging his head and shoulders onto my lap.

I gave him a light slap on the cheek because they always did that in the movies. If I'd had a glass of water, I'd have thrown that on him too. He groaned again but still refused to come all the way back to the land of the living.

I was already getting cold, so I couldn't imagine what condition this poor schmuck was in. There wasn't time to screw around anymore, so I reached toward his face, took my fingers, and forcibly opened his eyes.

"Wake up!"

His pupils constricted as the blinding light of the all-white winter day hit them, and his entire body flinched. His head snapped to the side, and he ended up with his face inches from my crotch.

Well, this is awkward.

"You in there? You coming around for me?"

The big man sighed, coughed, then swiveled his head so that he could stare up at my face.

"Am I dead?"

"Not yet." But if you hang around me long enough, you probably will be. "Can you get up?"

He shrugged his shoulders. "Not sure."

I felt him stretch, his muscles flexing as he tried to get his limbs working again. I really wanted him out of my crotch and tried to speed up the process by pushing him away. With my help, he sat up.

"You've got to stand up, pal. Freeze your pecker off out here in your underwear like this."

"Ah. Don't get much use for it."

"Your underwear?"

"My pecker."

I wasn't sure if that was a joke because he didn't smile or laugh, so neither did I. He rolled onto his knees and pushed up, climbing onto his feet.

As he stood there, his flesh almost blue, I realized he wasn't just half frozen. He was missing his left hand entirely.

"What the fuck happened to you?"

"That would be a long story."

"How about you try the short version."

"I'll get around to that. But first, I need you to help me find my dog."

Dog? The very sound of the word increased my heart rate by twenty beats per minute. Did this odd fellow actually have a dog or was he nuttier than a fruitcake? I told myself it was probably the latter. That, or he'd frozen part of his brain and was having some sort of delusion.

"You've got a dog?"

"Not dog. Prince."

Yep, the dude had lost it. And I really wanted to see a dog too. Damn it.

"Well, get in the Jeep, and we'll drive around and look."

He shook his head, his beard whipping from the defiant gesture. His eyes were locked on the woods around us. "Not going anywhere without him. I hurt him. Got to tell him—" He coughed, recovered. "I'm sorry."

I'd just driven a thousand miles and found an insane, almost naked man who was more concerned with a canine apology than freezing to death. My eyes scanned the forest, but all I saw were trees and snow. Certainly, no dog.

"Prince!" the man called out. "Prince! Come back, boy. I'm sorry. Christ almighty, I'm so sorry. I only did it to protect you."

He sounded panicked. He was more upset over the dog and whatever he'd done to it than his own pathetic condition. I watched him, his entire body shivering—more than shivering, quaking—like a full-body seizure, and I didn't know if it was the cold or anxiety or a combination of both.

It occurred to me again that this man might have gone insane. God knows the current state of the world could do that to a person. Should I really put my own life in jeopardy for him? Bad decisions in this world got you killed. Trusting people got you killed. Just ask LaRon.

Fuck it. That was enough. I wasn't a bad guy, no matter how many times I told myself otherwise. LaRon had made the decision to light them on fire. I'd given him other options, but he ignored me. It wasn't my fault. Shit happens.

I wasn't going to drive away this time. Even if it meant standing in the snow beside a guy in his tighty-whiteys hollering for a dog that probably didn't exist.

"Here, boy!" I called out. "Come here, boy. I've got beef jerky and canned sausages in the Jeep."

The man cupped his lone hand to his mouth and yelled louder. "Prince! Come back, and we'll go for a ride with—" He looked at me. "What's your name anyway?"

"Mead."

"Good to meet you, Mead. I'm Aben."

THE DOG DIDN'T COME. After twenty minutes of calling for it, Aben was shaking so violently I thought he might pass out and, if that happened, he was dead meat.

I convinced him to get into the Jeep. I turned the heater on full blast and watched as some of the color ebbed back into his skin. But the heat didn't linger, and I noticed Aben looking for the missing doors, the nonexistent roof.

"I th-th-think you could use a better ride for the season."

"Sorry about that. I got this back in June. Didn't really consider winter."

He nodded, too busy sucking down bottle after bottle of water to answer. I'd given him one of my denim shirts, but it was too small and gaped open at his chest. He was too large for any of my jeans or boots, but I'd brought an old quilt with me when I left the lodge, and I draped that over his lap and legs.

He still hadn't told me what had happened to get him into this predicament, and I held off on asking. He wasn't as loquacious as LaRon, at least so far. He had noticed the Gatling Gun still mounted to the roof and knew what it was. He seemed disappointed when I told him there was no ammo.

"Shame," he said. "There's someone I'd liked to have tried it out on." He didn't expound on that, and I didn't follow up.

Dusk was fast approaching, and I knew we should move on, but the desperation in Aben's eyes made me wait. I'd begun to believe that there was a dog, and, damn it, now I wanted to find it too. My mind raced as I tried to figure out how to make that happen. And then it dawned on it.

"Hey, I've got an idea."

Aben peeled his eyes from the tree line and looked at me. "What's that?"

"This dog of yours, is it protective?"

Aben seemed to consider it. "Saved me from some zombies more than once."

"Good. Then let's try something out."

A few minutes later, we were standing on the snowy road, and I was eager to see if my plan would work.

"Ready?"

Aben nodded.

I raised my fist. "You son of a bitch! I'm gonna kill you!"

I swung, missing by several inches, but Aben slapped his open palm against his exposed belly to create a ringing smack. Then he cried out in faux pain.

"Don't do it! Don't kill me, please!"

I imagine there was far superior acting in high school class plays, but I heard leaves rustle in the woods. Aben heard it too, and his head snapped in that direction.

"Not yet," I whispered. "Keep going."

He reluctantly turned back to me. I feigned another punch, and he dropped to his knees. "I'm sorry! Just don't kill me!"

"It's too late for sorry's, asshole!"

I grabbed him by the throat and pretended to squeeze. He made some of the fakest-sounding choking noises I'd ever heard, but less than five seconds into it, the dog hit me in the back.

I tumbled forward, crashing into Aben, bouncing off him, and falling into the snow. And then the dog was on top of me. I felt the heat coming off it as it snarled and growled, baring every one of the bright, white teeth in its jaws.

I crossed my arms in front of my face, and the dog latched onto my forearm with a shocking amount of pressure. It whipped its head back and forth, shaking my upper body. If I hadn't been suited up, that tan mongrel would have been having a Mead-burger.

Any time now, I thought. Call off your damn dog, Aben.

As if he'd read my mind, Aben appeared beside the dog and put his hand on its back. At his touch, the dog released me. It flinched, cowering away from the man. Its body was tensed, ready to run.

"Prince. It's okay, boy. It's okay. I'll never hurt you again."

He eased his palm down the dog's back, scratching its hind quarters, massaging it gently. I thought some of the fear had left the animal and risked uncovering my face.

"You're such a good boy, Prince."

I realized he was crying. I felt like crying too, and I didn't even know what the hell was going on. But Aben had his dog back, and I thought maybe, just maybe, I'd found new friends. And at the moment, that was all that mattered.

DECEMBER 3

"It still boggles my mind that you came along when you did. If we told anyone that story, they'd be apt to disbelieve it, and I wouldn't blame them."

We'd been driving south as quick as the roads allowed. By the time we got to Maryland, the snow was a thing of the past, the temperatures were gradually rising, and the more he warmed up, the more talkative Aben grew.

"It's like you were sent there by God."

I cast him a sideways glance. "I don't know about that. I doubt God has much use for people like me."

Aben looked at me, his eyes so intense that I couldn't hold his gaze for longer than a moment. "I wasn't even sure there was a God. But now, after that, how could I deny it?"

"Well, for whatever it's worth, I'm glad I found you."

Aben eventually told me his tale, starting with getting arrested not far at all from my former home in Johnstown to losing his hand, to the various survivors he encountered along the way. There were soldiers and sacrifices, secret government bunkers, and island villages.

The culmination, of course, was how he ended up almost bare ass on the roadway while being stalked by zombies. It was quite a tale, and from a different man, I might have suspected much of it was made up, but Aben seemed honest almost to the point of embarrassment, and I didn't get any sense that he was lying, or even exaggerating, his tale. I shared my story as well but might have massaged the facts a bit. Some things didn't need repeating.

We were on the same page that heading west was the best option, but three days into our journey, we had our first spot of trouble. We'd stopped at a grocery store to restock when I noticed Aben had forgone filling his cart with food and instead had a mixture of medical supplies. Gauze, antiseptic, bandages, and painkillers. I was still getting to know this man but thought it wasn't outside the realm of collegiality to inquire.

"Care to tell me what's up?"

He looked at the supplies in the cart, then back to me. "Think I got a bit of a problem."

"What kind of problem?"

"The frostbite kind."

He took a seat on a metal bench and took off boots we'd nabbed at a thrift store a few days earlier. I saw right away that the ends of his white socks were stained orangish brown, the color of pumpkin pie. The toe end was also much larger than it should have been, and I could smell the infection.

I knew this wasn't going to be good, and as he peeled off the socks, I was tempted to shout at him to stop. I didn't want to see this. But saying so would have been impolite.

Sometimes, it's okay to be impolite.

The horror show that was revealed when those socks came off was unlike anything I'd ever seen. The front end of his right foot was swollen twice its normal size, and the skin was a deep, chocolate brown. And that was the better of the two.

All of Aben's little piggies on his left foot were jet black, as was the skin on his foot a third of the way back. Where the skin transitioned from black to tan, there were a series of festering sores that leaked putrid ooze. Two hideous blisters that looked like small water balloons ready to burst rose up from his flesh.

"Oh... my."

Aben grunted. "That's a little worse than I expected."

"A *little* worse? Jesus Christ, that's the most horrible shit I've ever seen. And I've seen some horrible shit. What the fuck are we gonna do?"

Aben leaned back in the chair and looked out the window. "I am going to sit right here. Being that I'm impaired and all. You, on the other hand, are going to head to that hardware store over thereabouts." He pointed down the street.

"And why am I going there?"

He looked back at me, his face emotionless, his voice flat. "Well, to start off, we're going to need a saw."

I FOLLOWED Aben's instructions to the letter. I also killed three zombies, two on the way to the store and one on the way back.

Upon my return, I saw Aben had taken a pair of medical scissors and cut open the blisters. He pressed down on them with gauze, and thick, rust-colored infection drained onto the tile floor, forming a small puddle.

He looked up at me as I approached. "I decided to commence the party without you."

"I'm not even mad."

I sat across from him and displayed my haul. A battery-powered angle grinder with a cutting blade, some bungee cords, and two road flares. "I couldn't find the torch thing you asked for. The burnzomatic?"

Aben nodded. "I reckon those should suffice."

"Are you sure you can do this?"

Our eyes met. "No. That's why you're going to."

"I—"

"You saved me on the road. Once you save a man's life, you're responsible for him."

"I don't think that's how it works."

"Mead, if the dead parts of my foot don't come off, it's going to be a matter of days before the infection goes up my legs, and then I'm really gonna be in a pickle. I'm pretty sure I can get by on one and a half feet. But losing my legs..." He took a long swig from a bottle of wine and tilted it toward me.

"I think I better keep my head on straight."

"Probably wise."

I wanted to be drunk. Hell, I wanted to run off and leave him there to do this himself. He'd done it before with his own hand, after all. He should be a pro at self-amputation by now. But after losing every friend I'd found on the road, I figured I should do my best to keep this one alive.

"Anything else I need to do before we start?"

Aben pointed to Prince, who laid beside a bag of kibble from which he'd been eating. "Take him to the other side of the store and tie him up. He doesn't need to see this, and if I react poorly, he's liable to do the same."

I did as told, giving the dog an extra piece of beef jerky for listening so well. "You really are a good boy." I scratched his ear, and his tail thudded against the floor. "I'll do my best not to hurt your buddy, okay? I promise." He panted, happy and oblivious.

When I got back to Aben, he'd taken a brand-new leather wallet and held it to his mouth, ready to bite down. "One last thing."

"Yeah?"

"Once you start, don't stop until it's done, okay?"

"No coffee breaks in between?"

"I'd appreciate it if you not."

I knelt in front of him, almost like I was preparing to shine his shoes. If only.

"Ready?" he asked.

"Shit no."

"That's good. If you thought you were ready for this, I think I might begin to worry."

He smiled. I don't know how he worked out that expression knowing what was to come. Maybe it was the wine. Or maybe he really was that tough of a son of a bitch. Either way, it didn't make much sense to delay the inevitable.

We'd decided to try to treat his right foot, to hope that the nearly dead skin would somehow survive, but a good one-third of the left foot needed to be excised. Aben had even taken the time to draw a dotted line and above it, in small, neat printing, wrote, "cut here."

"Ready now?"

He didn't respond. He put the wallet in his mouth, bit down, and tilted his head toward the ceiling. No words were needed. It was time for me to do my job.

I jumped when I turned the saw on. The blade whirred fast and loud, and the sound reminded me of a dentist's drill. I almost stopped but knew dragging it out would only make it worse on Aben. And me.

The blade sliced through the skin on top of his foot with ease. A mixture of blood and infection as thick as cake batter drained out.

I didn't even have to push, only maintain light pressure, and the blade sunk deeper into his foot, through the tendons, and then it hit the bone.

Smoke rolled from the wound, and a dust containing minuscule particles of bone clouded around the surgery site. I could feel the grinder heating up due to the increased friction. And then downward movement stopped.

I looked. The foot was still there.

I panicked, confused, until I realized the four-inch blade only had two inches of clearance before hitting the center hub. I'd gone as deep as possible, and the only solution was starting all over again, this time from the bottom up.

I glanced up at Aben. Sweat dripped down his forehead, and I could see his teeth digging into the wallet. I needed to finish this fast.

Cutting from below was awkward, and I had to get on my belly to see what I was doing. Blood and pus and bone kicked back from the blade and splashed against my clothes and face. I thought I might puke but held it in because the dead part of Aben's foot was almost severed.

I pushed the grinder into the cut, using as much force as possible. The whirring, cutting sound as it sawed through the bone was unlike anything I'd ever heard before, and I felt another wave of nausea wash over me.

You can do it, I told myself. You have to do it. There's no going back now.

Once final push and the frostbitten part of Aben's foot tumbled to the floor. The black toes poked up at the air like some kind of Halloween prop. I dropped the grinder, and it kicked and spun before coming to a stop.

There was blood and pus everywhere, and more blood gushed out of Aben's wound by the second. I searched the area around me, trying to find the flares, but I'd lost them. I didn't know how it happened, but they were gone. I knew he could die if the wound wasn't cauterized, and it would be my fault. Again. Another death on my head.

I looked upward, toward Aben, just as a red glow filled the area around us. He had a flare in hand and the striker in his mouth. He spat that part free. "I got this now."

He held the flame toward the surgical site, and the fire cooked the skin. The smell was even worse than the cutting, and that time I did puke, but at least I managed to dash a few yards to the side before doing so.

When I returned, Aben was examining his new half-foot. He turned toward me. "Not too bad for your first time."

The end of his foot was charred black, but it had stopped bleeding. And somehow, it looked better than before.

"Why'd you take the flares?" I asked.

"I suspected you might pass out on me and didn't want to bleed to death,"

"But I didn't."

"You did not, and I much appreciate that. So much that I'll overlook the vomiting."

I glanced at the pile of puke in the corner. "I'll clear that up if you can handle..." We both looked at his severed foot and the gore surrounding it.

"Sounds like a plan."

DECEMBER 13

We remained in the store for over a week while Aben recovered from his amateur surgery. It was slow going, and he hobbled around with crutches most of the time so as not to put weight on the foot and break open the wound, but there were no signs of infection. His right foot also seemed to be on the mend, with some normal color coming back into the extremities.

On Aben's request, I'd made a few more trips to the hardware store. He wanted a double-bladed axe and more blades and batteries for the grinder. I watched as, over the course of a few days, he removed the sharpened edges of the axe head, grinding them down and smoothing them out until what remained looked like an oversized egg.

"Doesn't that defeat the purpose?" I asked.

Aben ran his hands over the hard end of the tool. "The Native Americans used to fasten rocks to the end of tree branches. I decided to put my own spin on that."

"But why cut off the edges?"

"The problem with bladed weapons is that they sink too far into the body and can become stuck. In hand-to-hand combat, you might not have time to extract said weapon. A blunt edge causes considerable trauma without that risk."

"Really?"

"That's the theory."

"Whose theory?"

"Mine."

Who was I to argue?

When it came time to leave, I was so focused on getting Aben to the Jeep without falling that I was oblivious to the presence of an approaching zombie until it was within a few yards of us. If it hadn't been for Prince growling, I most likely would have missed it even then, but the dog's low rumble alerted me that something was amiss.

I turned and spotted a middle-aged woman in a hotel maid's uniform. Her nose had been chewed away, as had her upper lip, giving me a good look at her crooked teeth. Thick, yellow drool ran out of that wound and dribbled onto her shirt.

"Wait here," I said to Aben. "I'll get one of the spears."

"That's not necessary." He pushed me aside with ease, then took a wobbly step toward the dead woman. She tried to snarl, but it lost much of the effect since she was missing her lip.

"Believe me, darling. I'm doing you a favor."

Aben had no weapons on him, or so I thought. It turned out that he didn't need one. When the woman got close enough, he swung his crutch like a bat and hit her in the temple. It connected with so much force that she wasn't just knocked sideways, flying a good five feet before crashing into the street.

The man looked back at me. "Problem solved."

DECEMBER 30

WE WERE NEARING ARKANSAS WHEN WE CAME ACROSS A motorhome sitting at the edge of a campground. That wasn't the most unusual sight, but nine zombies clawed at the side of the RV, trying clumsily to gain access.

"Think there's someone in there?" I stopped the Jeep ten yards from the scene.

"Someone or something. Odds are that it's just more zombies."

"Yeah." I watched the creatures as they banged against the motorhome. If the carrot red hair was any indication, four of them were members of the same family. Mom and dad zombies were both beanpoles, and their two brats, girls who looked to be about ten and wore their hair in matching pigtails, were equally slim. Even though they were dead, their freckles still stood out against their pale, gray flesh.

The other zombies were a mismatch. An elderly man in shorts that were much too short for his age and a pinstriped polo shirt. A beefy fellow in a jogging suit that clearly didn't get enough use. A woman with the kind of short, no-fuss hairstyle that always made me think the wearer was a lesbian. A teenage boy in a scouting uniform.

Rounding out the group was a little boy who couldn't have been more than four or five. That one got to me a little because he was close to the age of my own son. The kid was barely tall enough to reach the body of the RV, and his grubby paws scratched at the underside of the frame, desperate.

"We could keep on driving," Aben said.

"Yeah." I watched as one of the pigtail twins bumped onto the fat jogger. The larger zombie turned and smacked into her, knocking her to the ground, which stirred up a cloud of dust when she landed. She staggered to her feet, then returned to trying to get into the RV.

"We could. But then I'd always wonder,"

"Curiosity's a bitch."

"That it is."

'They're too close to the motorhome to use the wings. I'd be afraid of hitting it and breaking one off."

"You want to do this by hand?"

"I think that's for the best."

"Okay then."

I looked at him as he began to exit the Jeep. "You don't have to do this."

Through his wild, patchy beard, I think he smiled. "Now, where's the fun in that?"

Aben ordered Prince to stay, and the dog obeyed as we left the safety of the Wrangler and went to the zombies. I was armed with a spear. Aben limped along with his club in hand, but he also had a pistol tucked into his belt.

We weren't exactly quiet, but the zombies were preoccupied with whatever was inside the motorhome. I noticed it had "Born Free" painted on the side in a looping, delicate script.

The scout was closest to me, and when I got within striking distance, I rammed the spear into his ear so hard that it poked out the other side. He hung there for a moment, skewered in midair, then his legs gave out, and he fell.

With that, the other zombies realized there were easier targets than those inside the RV and came for us.

I tried to pull the spear free but only dragged the scout toward me. The jogger was getting close, and I jerked again, but the scout's shish kebab head moved in sync with the motion, and the spear remained stuck.

I began to panic and wished I'd gone with a sword or, better yet, kept driving, but Aben came up beside me, passed me by, and strolled up to the jogger. He didn't say a word as he swung the club.

The weighted end smashed into the jogger's skull with a sound like an egg cracking, only about a million times louder. I watched as the side of the jogger's head collapsed inward, pieces of bone and brain careening through the air as he dropped.

I couldn't believe the destruction that simple tool had wrought and couldn't stop myself from blurting out, "Holy shit!"

Aben glanced back at me. "Works even better than I'd hoped."

He continued forward and used the tool to destroy the toddler. The boy's head almost disappeared under the force of the club. I was glad he had taken care of that one, but there were six other zombies to deal with, and I couldn't let Aben, with his missing hand and half a foot, do all the hard work.

I put my boot on top of the scout's skull to hold it immobile and yanked the spear free. When I looked forward, I saw Aben kill one of the pigtail twins. The rest of the family was within feet of him. I knew this man was more than capable of handling himself, but I was done taking chances when it came to my friends, and I ran toward them.

I speared the remaining twin through the eye, careful not to push all the way through her head, then moved on to the carrot-haired mother. My aim wasn't the best, and I hit her in the mouth, breaking off one of her front teeth and stabbing deep into her throat. She gurgled up a few mouthfuls of black blood, then swatted at the spear, trying to free it. Aben put an end to that when he hit her from behind and caved in the back of her skull.

I speared the ginger dad in the temple, and he dropped like a stone. That left the possible lesbian and the old man.

"You have a preference?" Aben asked me.

I looked from one to the other, then back again. The old man's face reminded me of the whiny customers who would stomp to my station at the buffet and complain that the roast beef was too fatty or the turkey too dry when all I was doing was slicing the shit and slopping it onto their plates.

"I'll take the geezer."

"He's all yours."

The old man was even slower in death than he probably had been in life, and I was able to take my time as I decided where to stab him. I thought about going for his eyes or maybe aiming for one of the liver spots that covered his mostly bald head but decided to go for the center of the target.

I speared him through his bulbous schnoz, catching the tip almost dead on. The sight of the spear jutting from his nose as blood gushed out, like black water from a long unused faucet, brought a smile to my face. I jerked the spear side to side, up and down, and the geezer's time was up. When he fell, the spear came free.

I turned to see Aben standing over the possible lesbian, wiping his club off on her shirt. Her face was a puddle of black gore with bits of white bone floating in the soup.

"I enjoyed that," Aben said.

"It gets the blood flowing, doesn't it?"

"That's a good way to put it."

We moved to the entrance of the motorhome, and I let Aben man the door.

"Should I count down?" he asked.

I had the spear ready and shook my head. He opened the door.

And nothing emerged.

We waited ten seconds. Half a minute. Still nothing.

"You think maybe it's empty after all?"

I supposed it was possible. Who knew what made zombies do the things they did. Maybe they had smelled some gone-over mayonnaise or something equally banal.

"I'll go in," he said.

"No!" The word came out more forceful, bossier than I'd intended. I half expected him to punch me, but all he did was stand there.

"All right then. What's your plan here?"

I didn't have one. I just didn't want him going in there and possibly dying. I needed to do something, though, or else he might think me crazy.

"If anyone's in there, come out now. We killed the zombies. It's safe."

Aben raised his eyebrows, and I could read his mind. That's the best you got?

"Put down your weapons, please." The voice came from within the motorhome. It was feminine and calm. I couldn't detect any fear.

Aben gazed into the RV. "If it's all the same, I think I'll pass on that."

I thought there wasn't too much risk in doing what she had asked. If she had a gun, she'd have used it on the zombies, or us, by now. I set my spear on the ground. Then I moved a few yards back from the RV and motioned for Aben to join me. He did.

"You've got nothing to fear from us."

We waited, and soon enough, a woman appeared at the doorway. I guessed her to be about fifty, and she had long black hair with gray streaks running through it. Her face was tanned and hard and emotionless. "You boys put on quite a show."

"We try," I said.

She stepped out of the motorhome and came to us. "I'm Eloise."

"And I'm Aurora."

I looked past Eloise to see another female, this one in her seventies, at the door of the RV. She exited, and a third followed. She was younger, somewhere in her thirties, with a plain, broad face, and her name was Iris.

Just when I thought the show was over, a man on the downhill side of middle age emerged. He was Owen, and he had a fresh scar than started at his hairline and trickled down his face before ending near his upper lip.

Aben and I both watched the RV, expectant, and Eloisa gave a soft chuckle. "That's the entirety of us."

"How long have you been stuck in there?"

"Oh, only since last night. We ran out of gas and decided to sleep until morning. Before dawn, we heard them outside, trying to get in. I thought they might lose interest after a while."

"They're fairly single-minded," Aben said, and when I looked at him, I knew he was remembering his days on the snowy road, pursued by the ceaseless horde.

"We've got plenty of gas," I said. "You're welcome to it."

"That would be very much appreciated."

Aben and I, along with Eloise, Iris, and Owen, went to the Jeep to retrieve cans of gas. Only Aurora remained at the RV, and when I saw her walk, I realized why. Her back was stopped and twisted, and her head had a near-constant wobble.

I was in the process of handing Owen a five-gallon can of fuel when there came a sharp yelp from the direction of the motorhome.

We all turned and saw Aurora on the ground, a massive zombie towering over her frail frame. The woman crab crawled away from it, but her movements were slow and pained.

I don't remember making a conscious decision. All I remember was running. I had no weapons in hand, I wasn't even wearing my helmet, but I didn't care. I hit him from behind with all the momentum I'd built up in the sprint, and he tumbled headfirst into the RV.

I stumbled, hit the ground, but jumped back to my feet. Due to my increased focus on building my strength and stamina, I wasn't even winded. I grabbed a handful of the zombie's greasy, blond hair and slammed his face into one of the RV's wheels. There was a crunch as his nose gave way, and the monster gave a wet growl. I pulled him back and did it again. And again. And again.

He'd stopped moving, so I dropped him, his upper body hitting the ground with a thud. Then, I turned to Aurora and extended my hand. "Are you okay?"

"Not too bad for an old lady." She took my hand, and I lifted her gently. She gave my hand a hard squeeze. "You're my hero, and I don't even know your name."

I felt my face get hot and knew I was blushing. I couldn't hold back an embarrassed smile. "I'm Mead." And I kill the dead.

JULY, 3 YEARS LATER

AFTER THAT, I REALIZED THAT LIFE ON THE ROAD WAS TOO dangerous, that we needed to make a home we could secure and defend. We eventually found a small town named Brimley in northern Arkansas, which had two roads, one leading into it and one leading out of it.

The town contained only twenty or so zombies, and they were easy enough to kill. After that, we got to work on making Brimley secure. It turned out that Owen had been the one driving the motorhome and, in the life before the zombies, he'd been a heavy equipment operator. When I brought up building a fence, he was the one who suggested lining the town with shipping containers.

Over the next eight months, we secured the necessary machinery and enough metal containers to barricade the town two rows high. For coming and going, we turned a container on each end of the town sideways and reinforced the steel doors with extra metal, spikes, and barbed wire should the zombies, or maybe something worse, ever show up.

The town was far enough from any major, or even minor, cities that we didn't have to worry much. Every few days, a random zombie would stagger along, but it had no chance of getting into town and was easy to destroy with a well-placed shot from one of our lookout towers.

Every few weeks, a few of us left the safety of the walls in search of other survivors. We found a few. Not many, but three years in, our town had grown from six to eighteen. And we managed to keep all of them alive. Even Aurora, who is now 77 years old.

I'm not gonna lie. Spending most days inside a walled-off compound gets boring. There are only so many fields a man can plow and crops he can pick before the monotony sets in. Staying safe in the midst of the zombie apocalypse is easier than you think, but you sacrifice a piece of your soul in the process.

That's the worst part for me. That's why I go on every supply run, every scouting mission. I get my zombie-killing fix out there, in the wild, but there's a part of me that seems to get more anxious with each passing day. A part that longs for the excitement and the danger I'd experienced in the early months of the plague. Fear is a hell of a drug, and I haven't been scared in a long, long time.

EPILOGUE

THE PREACHER WORE A HOODED, WHITE ROBE THAT WAS SO LONG it sagged against the ground and the bottom few inches were stained brown. The sun baked down on him as he sat on a metal folding chair, an open bible in his hand. His lips moved, but no words came out as he read from the good book.

He sat behind an old, tattered tent large enough to hold over one hundred people, if said one hundred people were standing uncomfortably close together. That was the theory, anyway. In reality, he'd never witnessed more than two dozen people inside it.

Far from the tent, perhaps a mile or more away and out of sight, were his followers. He'd lost count of their number many months earlier, but it was in the thousands.

On the other side of the canvas barrier, voices leaked through the fabric. The sounds were a mixture of curious, excited, and skeptical. The preacher heard a few derisive comments but paid them no heed. By the time his sermon was over, there would be no unbelievers.

He was deep into the book of Revelation when a tent flap pushed open, and a woman's head peeked through the opening.

"It's time," she said.

The preacher placed a bookmark to keep his place, then closed the bible. He rose to his feet and set the book on the chair. He wouldn't need it.

As he moved toward the open flap, toward the woman, his robe threatened to gape open, but he cinched it tight before that could happen.

"Is everything okay?" the woman asked.

"Of course. Of course. God has given us another glorious day, and so nothing can be wrong." When he passed by her, he smelled stale cigarette smoke clinging to her but chose not to address that.

The preacher pushed through the flap and into the tent. He kept his face tilted down, hidden, but his eyes scanned the crowd. It was small, eight in all, but that was fine.

When he reached the pulpit, he paused, then picked up a small megaphone. He didn't need it for a group this small, but his voice had always been quiet, and it helped add power to his message.

"Thank you for your patience today, my friends. I'm pleased to see that you have found your way here through the grace of God."

The preacher saw two men in the back row tilt their heads together and whisper, but the other six watched, attentive.

"My ministry began a few years ago with the murder of my son. I wasn't aware at the time of his death why God had chosen to call my Josiah home, but after weeks of contemplation and prayer, it was all explained to me. Not only my son's murder. God told me why he allowed the plague to envelop our Earthly home. Why he allowed it to kill nearly every one of his children.

"Our country had grown wicked. We had turned our backs on God. Ignored his word. Spurned his unconditional love."

His voice grew louder, the timbre cascading, and his words came faster. Now he looked up at the crowd, and the hood slipped off his head. He heard them gasp, saw the horror on their faces, but that was good. That meant they were waking up.

"Our Heavenly Father needed to send us a message that was

impossible to ignore. To remind us that life was sacred again. For until we treat this life like the gift it is, we're cursed to damnation!"

All eyes were now trained on him. Glued to him. Rapt.

"God told me the truth! The dead, the zombies as you probably call them, are not to be feared. They kill only the wicked! The evil! The sinners!"

The preacher set the megaphone on the pulpit. He extended his arms to the side, and if there had been a cross behind him, it might have looked like he was being crucified.

The woman stepped out of the shadows behind him, took the soft fabric in her hands, and pulled it free from his body.

The crowd gasped. A few looked away. A woman in the front gagged.

In the back, Mead's eyes grew wide. He'd heard about this traveling tent revival from Duane Winningham, one of Brimley's latest arrivals, but he didn't quite believe it. Even with everything he'd seen over the last few years, this seemed too farfetched. Too impossible to be real.

But it was real.

The preacher stood at the head of the crowd, naked as the day he was born. A few deep scars had marred his face, but his body was far more deformed. His arms were covered solid with wounds and scars.

Some of the injuries were scabbed over, others fully healed. His torso was equally grotesque. A chunk of flesh the size of a tennis ball was missing from his abdomen, hollowed out and replaced by shiny, pink skin. A lesion on his hip was partially covered by a black scab that oozed pus and infection. The opposite thigh was half the size of the other, with great gobs of flesh eaten away and missing. That trauma was, mercifully, healed.

"Bring it to me," the preacher said, and the woman left the tent.

Because of Duane's story, Mead had an idea what was coming, but he squirmed, uncomfortable and nervous.

"This is fake, right?" Owen asked. He'd come along with Mead, who would have preferred to go to it alone but couldn't bring himself to say so.

"It sure as shit looks real to me."

"But he's not, you know, gonna let it happen?"

Mead didn't know what he thought and decided to keep his mouth shut and watch.

The woman emerged through the tent flap with a rope in her hands. A taut rope. As she continued into the tent, she moved closer to the preacher. When at his side, she handed him the rope. He accepted it and pulled it in toward himself, hand over hand.

A few seconds passed, the tension and anticipation building, and Mead thought the small, fragile-looking man was quite the showman. If this was indeed a show.

Mead's eyes drifted to the crowd which watched the preacher. He was looking at the woman in the front who had gagged a few moments before. Suddenly, her face twisted into a mask of confusion and fear, and she shrieked.

Mead returned his focus to the front of the tent where the preacher had reeled in a zombie. It was a man so black that its skin looked almost charbroiled. It was missing its left arm from the elbow down and had an old, unhealed bite wound on its face. The other end of the rope was tied around its neck. It looked toward the crowd, growling and snarling.

The woman who had screamed jumped to her feet and ran for the back of the tent.

"Wait!" the preacher ordered, and she stopped. "You have no cause for fear. You only think you do because you haven't yet realized the truth. This man, he cannot hurt you if you believe."

The preacher pulled the rope in further so that the zombie was almost within arm's reach.

"The undead, the ones who you call zombies, they are here to cleanse us! To consume our sins!"

The preacher dropped the rope and took the zombie's hand between his own. He pulled it toward him, stopping only when their bodies were touching. And then he did something that surprised Mead even more. He embraced it.

Everyone in the crowd had gone silent. Mesmerized.

The preacher looked into the zombie's face and gave a smile that Mead, even through his skepticism, thought looked sincere. "Show these people," he said to it. "Do with me what you will."

He released the zombie, and the creature stared at him, almost curious. Then, the zombie reached out with its lone hand and grabbed the preacher by the forearm. It pulled his appendage toward its mouth.

The preacher didn't react, didn't resist. He watched, serene, as the zombie bit down on his arm. It chewed off an oversized mouthful, swallowed, then took a second bite, like it was dining on a rack of ribs.

And then it stopped.

The zombie chewed on the excised flesh and looked up at the preacher, who laid his hand on top of the creature's shoulder.

"Thank you for saving me," the preacher said, and then he leaned in and kissed the creature on the cheek.

The woman picked up the rope and led the zombie out of the tent, and it went along without any protestations. The preacher returned his focus to the crowd, where everyone, even Mead, watched in amazement.

"Ladies. Gentlemen. As you can see, I am unharmed." Blood ran from his wounds, but he appeared at no risk of turning. "You've seen this miracle up close and in person. Few are so blessed to see God's glory firsthand. Can you say, 'Amen?'"

Most in the crowd responded, "Amen!"

"And now, I don't ask you for a donation, for your possessions. I don't want anything from you."

The woman redressed him in the robe, then stood at his side.

"I want you to believe because the ones who believe will be saved! The ones who believe will be impervious to danger! The ones who believe will find glory on this Earth as well as in Heaven!"

The preacher, whose given name was Grady O'Baker, walked

into the crowd. Mead realized they now watched him with something like adulation. "The ones who don't believe will burn in the fires of Hell for all of eternity!"

The woman, Juli Villarreal, came to Grady's side. Together, they dropped to their knees, clasped their hands together, and raised them over their heads.

"It is up to the believers to save humanity! I cannot do it alone, I need your help. And God needs your faith! So, I ask you, are you ready to believe?"

The crowd, including Owen but not Mead, shouted, "Yes!"

"Then pray with me now."

Apart from Mead, every man and woman in the tent joined the preacher, going to their knees and bowing their heads.

As Grady O'Baker led the others in prayer, Mead realized something. He was scared. More scared than he'd ever been before.

AFTERWORD

From the Author

Thank you! Thank you! Thank you!

I know this book was quite different from the others in the series, but I'd always planned on telling Mead's story, and what better way to do that than via his own words. I hope you enjoyed reading about his adventures as much as I enjoyed writing them.

The grand finale, Book 5 (Red Runs the River) is now available on Amazon. I hope you've prepared yourself because it's a wild ride!

If you've enjoyed the Life of the Dead books (and I sure hope you did), please take a moment to join my mailing list to receive news about the upcoming books in the series as well as my other books and stories. You'll also receive first chance at discounts and specials. http://eepurl.com/P8lc9

As an indie author, every review helps keep me writing. If you'd consider writing a review, it would mean the world to me. You can find links to all of my books on Amazon. https://www.amazon.com/Tony-Urban/e/B00HZ77O1O/

I continue to be blown away that the books I wrote in rural Pennsylvania are now being read all over the globe. Again, thank you for taking a few hours out of your life to take a chance on this book and on me!

I love hearing from readers, it absolutely makes my day, so if you'd like to reach out, please visit my website or send me a friend request on Facebook. The links are:

http://www.tonyurbanauthor.com

http://Facebook.com/tonyurban

Tell me about your favorite characters, your favorite scenes, and what you think will happen next!

And Happy Reading!